JESSICA FRANCIS KANE's first novel, *The Report*, was chosen as one of the Best Reads of 2012 for the Channel 4 TV Book Club. She is also the author of two story collections, *Bending Heaven* (Chatto & Windus, 2003) and *This Close* (Graywolf, 2013). She lives in New York City with her husband and their two children.

'Jessica Francis Kane's precise and moving *Rules For Visiting* is an altogether new sort of friendship novel, one about friendships stretched to their limits over time and space, the sort of friendships so many of us count as our closest. Kane's gift for describing beauty and loneliness, the real stuff of life, is unparalleled' Emma Straub, author of *The Vacationers* and *Modern Lovers*

'Crackles with wit' *New York Times*

'Reveals the power and limitations of modern-day friendships' *Evening Standard*

'Charming, lovely, funny and relevant' *Red Magazine*

'Jessica Francis Kane's novel will win your heart: single, melancholy, resourceful, May Attaway, the 40-year-old protagonist of *Rules for Visiting*, sets out on ̶ ̶ ̶ ̶ to rekindle her oldest friendships, and thereby to find herse̶ ̶ ̶ ̶ ̶ ̶ ̶ ̶ ̶ ̶ ̶ ̶ ̶ ̶ ̶ this gem of a novel celebrates t̶ ̶ ̶ ̶ ̶ ̶ ̶ ̶ ̶ ̶ ̶ ̶ ̶ e Messud, author of *The Burni̶ ̶*

'A witty, sometimes melancholy ̶ ̶ ̶ ̶ ̶ ̶ ̶ ̶ ̶ ̶ meditation on love, loss, friendship – and botany' *Wall Street Journal*

'Jessica Francis Kane has written a vivid, elegant and masterfully constructed novel about friendship and neighbours and our own personal odysseys. This is a deeply smart book, one I had difficulty putting down. There is real wisdom in these pages' Stuart Nadler, author of *The Inseparables*

Rules for Visiting

Jessica Francis Kane

GRANTA

Granta Publications, 12 Addison Avenue, London W11 4QR

First published in Great Britain by Granta Books in 2019
This paperback edition published by Granta Books in 2020
Originally published in the United States in 2019 by Penguin Press, an imprint of
Penguin Random House LLC

Illustrations by Edward Carey

A CIP catalogue record for this book is available from the British Library.

1 3 5 7 9 10 8 6 4 2

ISBN 978 1 78378 465 3
eISBN 978 1 78378 466 0

Offset by Avon DataSet Ltd, Arden Court, Alcester, Warwickshire, B49 6HN

Printed and bound by CPI Group (UK) Ltd, Croydon, CR0 4YY

www.granta.com

For Rachel, Rebecca, Laurie, Heidi, and Sharon
My original fortnight friends

Thus I visited each of my friends in turn,
trying, with fumbling fingers, to prise open their
locked caskets. I went from one to the other
holding my sorrow—no, not my sorrow but the
incomprehensible nature of this our life—for
their inspection. Some people go to priests;
others to poetry; I to my friends . . .

—VIRGINIA WOOLF, *THE WAVES*

Rules for Visiting

Departure

A problem: If you're in an airport on a moving walkway, and a stranger glides by on the opposite walkway holding a book bag printed with a phrase you've been thinking about for months, how long will it take you to finish the sentence? You have no frequent flier miles, an unprecedented amount of paid time off work, and a new rolling suitcase named Grendel.

A best friend is someone who . . .

The book bag in question was blue canvas and the words were printed in white. I thought the sentence might finish on the other side, the side pressed against the woman's ample hip, and that it might be important for me to figure out what it said. My eyes widened at the thought because at that precise moment I was on my way to visit a friend, Lindy, whom I hadn't seen in several years. If I had a best friend, and I wasn't sure that I did, I was on my way to see her.

I wish I could say I turned and ran in the wrong direction on the track in order to confront the woman and read the rest of her bag, but that would be cinematic. And by that I mean movies make the most of situations like this but life rarely does.

I looked over my shoulder just as my moving walkway came to an end, nearly tripping myself and the young mother behind me. I apologized, she swore at me from behind her stroller (the child was young, and, I hoped, deaf), and I rolled my suitcase off to the side, out of pedestrian traffic.

The air smelled of coffee, perfume, a little chlorine. There was something summery about it, which was at odds with the gray December sky visible through the airport skylights. The owner of the book bag was a heavyset woman in leggings and a Christmas sweater, and she wasn't moving very fast. She had a cell phone in one hand, a coffee in the other, and was tipped slightly to the side in an effort to talk on the phone and keep the bag from sliding off her shoulder. I'm almost forty and fit, mostly from gardening, and would not have had trouble catching her.

I would have had trouble explaining I needed to read the other side of her bag. What if it turned out to be nothing but corporate swag? "A best friend is someone who . . . buys you Gardenite shears."

Or a health advisory? "A best friend is someone who . . . gets a flu shot."

While I was considering other, worse possibilities, a child stopped in front of me. "Excuse me," she said solemnly, though large red bows held her hair up in very high pigtails. Most people smile at small children, but you really don't have to. They appreciate seriousness.

"Yes," I said.

"Excuse me," she said again.

"I'm listening," I reassured her.

But she turned to look behind her, toward a woman across the concourse in line for the family restroom, who was wrestling with an infant in a pouch across her chest. She frowned in our direction and waved in a way that suggested perseverance.

The child turned back to me. "Please?" she tried. "I'm thirsty."

I looked over my shoulder, then slid sideways so she could drink from the fountain I'd been blocking. When I looked up, the woman with the book bag was gone.

It is not like me to search for truth on the bags of strangers, but I was having an unusual year.

A few variables. Consider the word *visit*. It's from the Old French *visiter,* which meant "to inspect, examine, or afflict." You can visit a neighbor or a friend, but so can plagues and pestilence.

And *travel.* It's from the Middle English *travailen,* which meant originally "to toil or labor; torture."

So clearly traveling to visit friends should not be done lightly. There is a reason I named my suitcase after the first monster in English literature. Beowulf's Grendel traveled off the moors to visit Heorot because he wanted to stand listening outside the great hall of friendship. Shall I tell you that I know something of how he felt? I may not eat anyone, but transformations are not always violent or even physical.

O Muse. I sing of visits and the woman.

Yew (*Taxus baccata*)

— A Crossroads —

Midway through my fortieth year, I reached a point where the balance of the past and all it contained seemed to outweigh the future, my mind so full of things said and not said, done and undone, I no longer understood how to move forward. I was tipped backward and wobbly, my balance was off, and this made sense to me. A life seemed so long, I couldn't see how anyone proceeded under the accumulated weight of it.

Medication helped, for a while. Mainly I recall it giving me for a few months a pleasant sense of the present. I went to Washington, D.C., for a landscaping conference around that time and I remember with fondness the new and sudden ease of my morning routine. The edges of everything seemed clearer. And I don't mean just the lovely things like trees and the sunrise and the flowering kale (genus *Brassica*) planted everywhere in that city, but tubes of toothpaste and pots of face cream. It was easier to wash my face in the morning. In fact, it was a pleasure. I believed again in the possibility of a new day, the present one and the next one after that.

The facts of my life seemed clearer to me and I was able to think about them with a new kind of resolve. Not a resolve to do better; just a steady sense that this was the way things stood and it wasn't necessarily a catastrophe:

I have no hobbies and no desire to develop one.

I read books, but not always the best ones. I often say I like biographies, but in truth I rarely finish them, the last part of the life, the descent toward death, too depressing.

I am not a good cook.

I cannot sing and no longer play an instrument.

I am neither an early riser nor a night owl, so can claim no virtue in those realms.

Animals tolerate me but are not drawn to me.

The same is true of children.

I worry about the world but have never given much time to charitable work.

I cannot paint or speak a foreign language.

I own one cat, Hester, who is undeniably lonely.

I have not traveled much, a particular disappointment given my surname, Attaway, an Old English name that derives from the words for "at the way" and referred to someone who lived close to the road. Somewhere on the misty moors of England when naming began, a few people looked around and saw trees (Ash) or a whole stand of them (Ashworth) and named themselves accordingly. Others considered the work they did (Smith, Potter, Mason), or the town they were near (Walls). But my ancestor looked around and was inspired by the road, a means of travel and change. She must have stood "at the way" just as I stand on the bridge over the train tracks near my house in Anneville, turning north, then south, wondering about the possibilities in each direction.

I WORK AS A GARDENER for the university, which was certainly not what I'd planned. The first plants I remember tending were a series of African violets that suffered and died on my childhood windowsill. Their velvety leaves hate water, but I poured indiscriminately. Next there was a red geranium that lasted as long as it could (about two weeks) in the shade of my bookshelf. I don't know who gave me these plants or why I so glaringly neglected them; I was otherwise very careful about looking after my room. When the plants died, I remember carrying them out to the compost pile by the garage, each gloomy procession giving me the distinct impression I did not have a green thumb.

In college I kept a few dusty dorm plants; then, briefly in New York City, my studio apartment didn't get enough light to grow anything green even if I'd tried. But when I moved back to Anneville, something changed. Suddenly I wanted a whole garden. Years later it was pointed out to me that *guardian* and *garden* share a root meaning "safety, enclosure." I had come home, in part, to help care for my mother. I started reading gardening books and drawing plans. I was enthusiastic and optimistic, and if I was neglecting other aspects of my life (such as finding a job or my own apartment), I thought the payoff would be armfuls of flowers that would make us all feel better.

It didn't work out that way, but my interest survived and I eventually applied to the Landscape Architecture program at the university. Landscape architects are responsible for creating pleasing natural environments for people to enjoy. It could be a backyard or a park, a campus or a playground, a public road, highway, or parking lot. We're taught to carefully analyze the terrain to be planted, then create a design that works in harmony with everything around it. I completed two years, then took a job with the grounds crew at the university. It turned out I was less interested in designing spaces for other people than in working with the plants myself.

The job suits me, and I like working with Susan Mint, with whom I am often paired by our boss, Blake O'Dell, for bed maintenance around the university grounds. Sue is about a decade older than I am and prides herself on never having had an indoor job. "I started raking leaves as a kid to supplement my allowance," she told me. "Never looked back."

Sue and I go days talking about only the work at hand, but occasionally she has more to say, and by that I mean I don't know if we're friends, but she's a good coworker. She has a sense of humor I enjoy. Once, describing a garden designer we both know, she said, "She has a tendency to overdesign. I mean, she draws in her eyebrows, for god's sake."

Now Sue said, "I had a weird dream last night." We were raking the beds around the English Department, disturbing the little spring weeds. "I had my own landscaping company and a friend wanted me to landscape her yard." Sue stretched her back. "But she wanted a local stream redirected across her property and through her living room."

I stopped raking. "What?"

"Yeah, I know. At first I worried about damage to the watershed, too. Of course. But the more I thought about it, the more sense it made."

I waited.

"Watersheds are threatened everywhere, right? So bring them into your home to protect them. That was the idea, anyway, and somehow it made sense in the dream. I cut the path in a curve and used bluestone to build the banks. I even put in a small cascade. It was beautiful, but news of the project spread and then everyone wanted the same thing."

"That's terrible."

Sue nodded. She has strong forearms from years of gardening. A dusting of soil coated the skin visible between the top of her floral work gloves and the pushed-up sleeves of her black T-shirt.

"What was the name of your company?" I asked.

"I don't know. It didn't have one."

I didn't know what else to say, and Sue looked as if she regretted sharing the dream. We both went back to raking.

THE IDEA TO VISIT MY FRIENDS began with an article I read that spring in the book section of the newspaper commemorating the anniversary of the death of the writer Amber

Dwight. On a March afternoon fifteen years earlier, a plane carrying Amber and her parents had crashed into a mountain in North Carolina. She was on a tour promoting her first novel and her father, who had a small plane pilot's license, had been flying her around the country to her events. There were no survivors.

Immediately after her death the outpouring of grief from her friends around the country was enormous. A popular web magazine had created a site where people who knew Amber could share memories. And—this is important—it was before the advent of Facebook and Twitter and the page had been set up for posts only. For months people shared beautiful stories, and no one could like or judge or comment. The site was still up and you could read through the posts and come to your own conclusions, without cacophony. There was a quiet elegance to it, a hushed quality, missing from today's internet.

Most of her friends were writers of one kind or another, so their various remembrances and elegies were bound to be well written. Still, it was obvious reading through the site that there had been something extraordinary about Amber. There were stories about her generosity, her loyalty, her sense of fun and adventure, her expertise on everything from used-car parts to brownie recipes. She was very opinionated, but everyone seemed to agree that the opinions were well informed, insightful, and usually for the benefit of someone else's problem. People wrote that to meet her was a historical event, one you would remember for the rest of your life.

The article was accompanied by a black-and-white photo of

Amber, and I wondered if it had been her author photo. She was looking straight at the viewer, her head tilted, not smiling but not unsmiling either. She looked like she'd been a good listener.

> Amber was the campfire around which a lot of people gathered. And the amazing thing was that the people on either side of you, also huddling close to Amber? They might change your life, too. She created possibility of all sorts. —Helen

I read the site through from beginning to end, then went back to the beginning and read it again. My fascination rapidly became disappointment that I hadn't known her. We grew up in different states, but from the posts I learned we'd arrived in New York City the same year, the same month. While I was surviving alone on ramen noodles and taking endless walks in Central Park because I couldn't afford to do much else, she was apparently hosting notorious dinner parties, not because she was wealthy but because her life seemed charmed. But that's not fair. Maybe it was charmed, but she also seemed to be kind and made things happen.

> I've lived in the same building for ten years and still don't know the woman across the hall from me. Amber knew all her neighbors, and there was always some fun connection, like the guy downstairs, who was able to get her the orange paint she wanted for her living room because he was a set designer, or the

woman upstairs who was teaching her how to sew.
One year I tried to copy her—I made banana bread and
gave my neighbors poinsettias at Christmas—but it
didn't have the same effect. No one created a friendly
neighborhood as effortlessly as Amber. —Claire

Amber was befriending the neighbors and painting her
apartment fun colors while I was struggling to do my laundry.
I'd missed out on something, and I wasn't surprised. I have always
assumed others have more and better friends. Amber was
an extraordinary friend to many people and I wished I'd been
one of them, even if it meant sharing now in the acute pain of
the community she'd created.

What was obvious in post after post was that Amber had a
talent for friendship, which, I suddenly understood, was something
one could be good at, like cooking or singing. You could
be good at being a friend, and no sooner had I had the thought
than I knew I was not. I had some friends, but did I have a community?
No. Would a group of us someday rent a beach house
together and have a weekend of frivolous yet somehow poignant
fun? Never. Most of my friends do not know one another,
and even if they did, I'm certain they would not consider me the
center of anything.

As I read over and over again the stories of Amber and her
character, I tried to imagine myself writing something similar
about one of my friends. Or one of them writing about me. I
thought of my oldest friend, Lindy, a woman I've known since

seventh grade. We'd played soccer together in high school, were both in the orchestra, and once had a ferocious argument about whether hot fudge or strawberry topping at Dairy Queen was healthier. We went to different universities, and while I eventually moved back to our hometown, she never did. I see her now and then when she comes back with her children to visit her parents, but we aren't in touch regularly. I know her to be a kind and creative person who would probably be happy to hear from me if I picked up the phone and called her tomorrow. I consider her a friend based largely on our shared past, but do I really know her? Are we friends or just two people whose paths crossed in childhood, when bonds are more easily formed?

> I knew Amber for one day. Our publicists paired us for a book signing, so we met for coffee before the event. I haven't found many lasting friends since junior high or high school, but I liked Amber right away. I had this feeling we might become friends, that we would become friends, if it was okay with her. I'm heartbroken that that possibility is gone. —Elizabeth

Duck Woods

I live with my father, Earl Attaway. He is eighty and I'm his oldest child. Some years ago, he lost his son, my younger brother, to the West Coast. That is how we say it, a typical locution of my family, meant to make light of the fact that my brother moved far away and never visits. Attaways excel at euphemism.

My father built our house on Todd Lane the year he turned forty, the year I was born, his only act of practical construction in an otherwise wholly intellectual life. While the house was under construction, my parents lived next door, in the small bungalow now owned by our neighbors, the Fords. I prefer that house, but my father built a two-story brick Colonial for himself and my mother because that was a design admired when they were newlyweds and he wanted to build one. An academic, he wanted to lay bricks. He wanted to work with his hands. It is still the largest house in a neighborhood just now beginning to gentrify. Houses that have survived years of benign neglect are being freshly painted in historically appropriate colors. Yards that have never known anything other than a push mower now have professional plantings and crushed gravel paths.

I'm a gardener, so theoretically it should make me happy to see all this interest people are taking in their yards. Except it doesn't because they aren't; hired landscapers do all the work. To have an interest in gardens without gardening is like having an interest in food without eating. Most of my neighbors just want their property to look nice, that's all. They want perfect grass, and neat mulch skirts around their trees, and garden beds with color and texture but all of it easy to care for, which means the same four or five evergreen shrubs (genus *Juniperus* and *Thuja,* for the most part), mixed with a bit of azalea and hydrangea, maybe barberry and an ornamental grass, planted in repeat groupings. My boss, Blake O'Dell, calls it "LM," for low maintenance. The other day I passed a house where an ambitious gardener had gone out on a limb and worked some deep red day lilies (*Hemerocallis*) into the design. It was a good idea, but my first thought was, Those will be gone as soon as the homeowners realize they should be deadheaded daily to maintain a tidy appearance.

Our neighborhood is called Duck Woods, though I have never seen a duck and there are no woods. It's triangular in shape, bounded by a railroad on one side, a fast road—by which I mean the speed limit is thirty-five but everyone does fifty—on another, and a river on the third. My father says the area was originally Duck's Woods, named for an old family in town, and that may be true. No one ever remembers where to put an apostrophe so the *s* was probably lost over time. The whole area is two miles from the university and just rural enough for chickens, but not rural enough for bonfires; urban enough for sidewalks, but not urban enough for apartment buildings or semidetached houses; suburban enough for everyone to need a car, but not suburban enough for a homeowners' association to arise and impose maintenance standards.

My father knows everyone on Todd Lane. He often leaves flowers on doorsteps and treasures the thank-you notes he gets in return. He uses plastic milk jugs for vases, pulling them from the bins at the recycling center. There's been a story in the paper about it. He cuts off the tops of the jugs, fills them with water and flowers from our weed-choked garden, and sets out, sloshing water everywhere, down his beige pants, onto his white tennis shoes. I asked him once why he couldn't use jam jars or something smaller. His answer:

"If you had children, May, you'd know folks don't want glass on the doorstep. A child could knock it over and get hurt."

I know our street in a different way. I know that sometimes it takes the UPS truck half an hour just to go from one end of the street to the other because Todd Lane is full of people in what is called the "purchasing stage" of life: young couples with kids or kids on the way. The boxes range from Pottery Barn to Walmart, but inside the stuff is all the same.

Duck Woods is a perfect study in the intimacy of half-acre lots, and it isn't all shared jokes and borrowed baking ingredients. There's the house that overdecorates for Halloween and the house that overdecorates for Christmas. There's the house that keeps chickens and the house that keeps a dog outside too much. Across the way and two houses toward the bridge, there's a woman who has given a section of her yard to a refugee who grows his family's vegetables there. Meanwhile, across the way and three houses down, there's a woman who desires a garden worthy of the Anneville spring tour, and is thus waging a desperate effort to conceal the telephone pole in the middle of her backyard—placed there for a through road that was never built—behind a ring of Hicks yews (*Taxus x media "Hicksii"*), which will grow only to a height of about ten feet, and therefore hide the pole only for those with the vantage point of a hedgehog. Four doors down from her is a family slowly converting their entire yard into a paved play space for their children. Whether this is to save on landscaping costs or a hope that their son will someday play in the NBA, it's hard to tell, but the sound of a basketball bouncing on an inexpertly laid court fills the neighborhood most evenings. The wife is skilled at container gardening and says she feels blessed not to have any trees in her yard. She serves as the head of a group that wants to cut down an old oak near a playground on campus. The oak is healthy, but the long perpendicular limbs extending over the play equipment worry her. Arborists have attested to the strength of the wood, other parents have signed a petition saying they enjoy the shade, but she believes it is better to be safe than sorry. The UPS truck stops at her house more than any other, by which I mean it's a short step from ordering everything online to wanting to butcher an old tree for no good reason.

Three houses on our side toward the bridge is a woman who keeps five cats indoors and feeds the birds outdoors. I never walk by without seeing three or more of those cats staring morosely out the window, which does not make me sad because my heart is firmly on the side of the birds. I keep Hester inside, too. I do wonder what her house smells like, though. Two doors from us in the other direction is a young family with plastic play equipment always strewn about their lawn, never picked up, the pinks and purples now sun faded. At some point they spray-painted their camellia bushes silver; a project for the children or an attempt at gardening, I don't know. The house on the corner has wind chimes that sound like dishes being washed, and the other corner house has a private yoga studio in the back that violates the zoning code for this neighborhood, but the only person who might care about that is the woman striving for the garden tour, and since the yoga instructor also has a beautiful bed of roses on her front lawn, she has never said a thing.

The variety of human creativity expressed in landscaping isn't always a pleasure, but it is a wonder.

I try to be a good neighbor. I have never left a pumpkin out past Thanksgiving or Christmas lights up past the first of the year. The backyard is overgrown, true, but I keep the front under control. I rake the leaves and shovel the walk and throw down salt to melt the ice. I know my father tends to keep the neighbors talking for long periods of time and most of his conversations find their way back to World War II or growing tomatoes. He tires people with stories about who used to live in their houses forty, fifty years ago. Everyone seems interested at first, but how many times can you pretend to be impressed by the fact that Mrs. Profitt raised nine children in the two-bedroom bungalow you consider a starter home and plan to live in only until you have another child and move across town to the bigger houses and better schools?

I suppose people like my father out of some sense that it is right to honor the past. No one says "Negro" anymore, but no one tries to grow a ripe tomato from seed by the Fourth of July anymore either. His age earns him the right to startle people with his vocabulary and hobbies while their babies nap or idle in strollers or tear about the lawn. Like an old cat who drools, he is forgiven. He is ending his life on this street; they are starting theirs. If they notice this framing, they think it poignant. Not for one second do they think they might end their lives here, too, in such modest surroundings, on such a narrow road, on the wrong side of the railroad tracks from the university.

Fifteen years ago my father converted our basement into a walk-out apartment and gave the rest of the house to me. I suggested swapping. It was clear by then I was back to stay, but I wanted the basement, he could have the house. He refused. So I moved into the room that had been my brother's. My old room was not an option.

— El Puerto —

One of my friends in Anneville owns Santos's Garage. Leo Santos respects the care I give my car, a blue Taurus I call Bonnie, and I admire his work, as well as the large banner over the door that announces A WOMEN-FRIENDLY BUSINESS. Leo also owns the Mexican restaurant, El Puerto, at the end of the Wayside strip mall. His parents came to this country when he was six. His father opened the garage and it was his mother's idea, after observing how women were treated at other garages, to put up the sign. Santos's did so well, Leo moved his parents to a house just outside of town when they were ready to retire and still had money left over to buy a struggling burrito place and turn it into El Puerto, a nice taqueria.

Leo is kind and honest and his hours are reliable, unlike Mrs. Kim, the owner of Kim's Convenience at the other end of Wayside. She repeatedly closes early and will not open the door, even if you point out the time. When some kids spray-painted "In" in front of "Convenience" last summer, I wasn't as sorry as I should have been.

Leo says the formula for getting through the week in a small town in a modest job is rhythm and routine, and I think he's onto something. My routine includes a burrito twice a week at El Puerto, once on Monday after work by myself, and again on Thursday with my father after he gets home. He's an emeritus professor now, but the university gives him a little closet of an office he still goes to on Thursdays. Leo calls my father "the English professor" and my father calls Leo nothing after I told him "the Mexican mechanic" wasn't appropriate.

"It's a joke."

"But Leo is Mexican."

"Just 'the mechanic,' then?" my father asked.

"But he's also a cook," I said.

I'm fond of Mexican food and El Puerto is within walking distance of my house. It's nice to know I can enjoy a beer or two with my dinner and not have to worry about driving home. The restaurant looks out over the Wayside parking lot, which isn't a great location, though a parking lot view is common in Anneville, as everywhere. We build them for maximum capacity, so most of the time these seas of asphalt, useful to no living organism, just bake in the sun. Actually, parking lots are useful to reporters, who seem to have no trouble finding in them people to interview. Approach the same person at home in their yard, and they'd probably run you off. Get someone standing next to their SUV at Costco, and they'll make pronouncements about anything.

Leo and I are the same age and, like me, he cares about what things are called. He dislikes the term "strip mall," for example. He prefers "shopping center," and he's not wrong. Many residential developments give themselves beautiful names not based on reality; why shouldn't strip malls do the same? In Anneville we have The Cliffs (there are no cliffs in town), Citrus Grove (wrong climate; we are USDA Plant Hardiness Zone 7), and a retirement complex called Sunrise View, though the majority of its windows face west. I was encouraged when a new development called Stonegate Apartments was announced.

"Now, that's achievable," I told Leo.

"But people want aspirational," he said.

As American strip malls go, Wayside is not bad. It's old-fashioned in the sense that the signs are all different colors and typefaces rather than coordinated. Parking lots are sometimes landscaped with small trees—crepe myrtle (*Lagerstroemia*) is popular—and I will always park near one when I can, like a rabbit aiming for a copse in a cleared field. But the Wayside lot doesn't have any. The land behind it, however, descends into a hollow, a lovely partially wooded dell, where the air is always cooler and flocks of birds fill the trees. I often hear starlings chattering away in there. On the far side of the hollow the land rises to the edge of Duck Woods. Years ago someone must have scattered a wildflower seed mix in the meadow because there are some nonnative species that thrive until the city mows in the fall. The whole dell, meadow plus the wooded area, isn't much larger than a football field.

In May, a crew with construction equipment spent a day breaking up a sizable portion of the parking lot in front of El Puerto. People made political jokes—"Building your own wall? *El pequeño muro?*"—but I thought it must be a water or gas main problem. Then a banner went up that said OUTDOOR DINING COMING SOON!

I recognized Leo's work. Later I learned he'd gotten permission to extend his dining area outside by giving up the parking spaces in front of the restaurant and paying a small municipal fee. His vision was to create the feel of sidewalk dining, which existed elsewhere in town, mainly on campus, where the fancier restaurants are. He did most of the work himself and within a few weeks the area in front of El Puerto had a low wooden deck with tables hugging the restaurant and a high counter with stools facing the parking lot. He installed some lights around the area and bought red table umbrellas and votive candles. He has a good sense of design and the result was nice, surprisingly elegant for a strip mall. He named it "El Puerto Promenade," and when he opened with a free taco night, the line stretched all the way across the parking lot.

― The Taurus ―

There's a place in Anneville, the light at the corner of University and Main, where I can put Bonnie in neutral, take my foot off the brake, and she won't move forward or backward, not one inch, because it is absolutely flat. I pointed this out to my father on our way to El Puerto on the last Thursday in May. I'd picked him up at his office because his car was in Leo's garage. He seemed interested in my observation, but then behind us someone's tires squealed and he said something odd.

"Never has a country so in love with the automobile driven it so poorly."

I braced myself. My father has a way of making the universal feel personal. "What do you mean?"

"We no longer really walk anywhere or sail." He cleared his throat, and I wondered if he'd been planning this speech. "The spirit of flying is dead, space exploration is a joke. Our affair with the car, however, continues. The names alone express all our hope for adventure and riches. Look at that."

We were behind an Expedition. In front of us, one lane over, was a Sable.

"And the Taurus?" I asked. "That's not a particularly glamorous name." I popped open the sunroof.

"What's that?"

"This car, a Ford Taurus."

He looked at me. "Your car is a Taurus? Like the zodiac sign?"

"Yes. So is yours, but I have the sedan."

"The sign of the bull."

"I thought you knew that."

"I did not."

"My first car was a Fiesta. Fiesta, Taurus, next a hybrid, I hope. Those are the cars I have owned."

"'Ask me for my biography and I will tell you the books I have read.'"

I knew from his tone he was probably quoting someone. I turned on the radio. He has said before that I pay too much attention to my cars, by which he means I should marry and have a family. But is the American Dream more house or car? Is it putting down roots or being able to move? Most people can't decide.

"How's the English professor?" Leo asked when we walked into El Puerto. He called out to the kitchen my father's usual—a pinto bean burrito with extra guacamole—and escorted us to a table.

"Fine . . . sir," my father said after a quick glance at me. Then he bowed, and Leo, smiling, bowed back.

"Do you know he's impervious to poison ivy?" my father said as Leo walked away.

"How do you know that?"

"He told me. We do occasionally speak when you are not around."

I opened my menu and my father pulled an envelope out of his breast pocket. Inside was a thank-you note from—judging from the penmanship—one of the kindergarteners on the street.

"Bella," he said, showing it to me. "And her little brother, Henry. I gave them some coneflowers from the garden."

By garden, my father meant the bed behind the house that I'd started years ago and now ignored. Certain of the hardier perennials, echinacea among them, continued to thrive amid the weeds.

"Very nice," I said, handing the note back.

"They're our neighbors."

I knew that. I also knew that Bella and Henry's mother, Janine, often stood in her front yard eyeing the Norway maple (*Acer platanoides*) in her yard, my favorite tree on the block. It's holding on to a lot of dead wood—Norway maples die slowly from the top down—and for that reason stands out like a battle-hardened warrior on our leafy street. I wish it were in front of our house because I would never cut it down. Janine's thoughts on trees I can't read.

"Are they?" I said.

My father frowned and we ate salsa and tortilla chips for a few minutes without talking. For an old man, my father eats neatly, which is a blessing.

Many of our neighbors on Todd Lane, like Janine, arrived within the past five or six years. But some have lived on the street much longer than that, by which I mean they probably have memories of me as a child. And yet we rarely greet one another with more than a wave. And that's fine because, frankly, when do you work into a conversation the difficult details of your life? Am I supposed to give them all the information for their benefit, to explain my eccentricities? Maybe I should put up a sign? Yes. Let's all have signs up and down the street announcing our personal disasters and disappointments. That would be helpful, perhaps even neighborly.

"We live in close proximity, that is true," I said.

Ash (*Fraxinus excelsior*)

I n my mailbox the next evening I found a photocopied picture of an ash tree (*Fraxinus excelsior*) with a question mark in the upper-right-hand corner. The ash is native to the British Isles and is particularly vigorous on limestone rocks, since it tolerates calcium in the soil. Ash seeds are called keys because they resemble keys used for medieval locks, and the tree's branching crown is always open, with ample space between the limbs and twigs. The wood is preferred above all others for the handles of hammers, axes, shovels, chisels—any tool subject to sudden shocks and strains.

In many ways, the ash presents an ideal model for a family tree.

I separated the photocopy from the rest of the mail and added it to the stack on top of the microwave. This was the archive of my father's memorial tree research. He hopes the university will plant a tree in his honor before he dies, but if that doesn't happen, the plan is for me to designate one privately. The pressing question: What kind?

My father has been giving me these photocopies, his tree sheets, for three years.

— The Yew —

When Leo opened his promenade in June, the news made the paper's restaurant section. In July, a poet in the English Department won the world's richest prize for a single poem—fifty thousand dollars. That made the front page. The poem was about a yew (*Taxus baccata*) in one of the university gardens and the paper reprinted the poem alongside a photograph of the tree. Our grounds crew—which at that moment consisted of me, Sue, Blake O'Dell, and five college students working summer jobs—sat at a picnic table on campus and read it over lunch. Blake couldn't see it very well from the far side of the table, so when Sue and I were done, we pushed it over to him. She and I chewed quietly while he read. Then, when he was done, he pushed the paper down to the students at the end of the table, and he chewed quietly until they were done.

The poem was titled "The Darkling Yew" and it had 4 stanzas, 32 lines, and 166 words. I know that because Sue got the paper back from the students and counted them all out loud. When she was done, Blake looked up at the clouds for a moment and said, "That's in the neighborhood of three hundred dollars a word."

One of the students at the end of the table whistled.

"I remember when you put that cutting in," Blake said.

"I was just thinking about that," I said.

"I recall thinking it wasn't such a good idea."

"You didn't."

"Foliage that contains highly toxic alkaloids at a peanut-free university." He smiled. "Seemed like asking for trouble."

"It was. But we put the sign up."

He nodded. "And it's too close to the wall."

"The wall *is* compromised in that section," Sue said. "The roots are up under it. Architecture complains every year. I guess they won't anymore."

The picture of the yew that accompanied the story was very poor. It is a dark and mysterious tree native to Europe and Great Britain, but the newspaper's grainy black-and-white photograph, which appeared to be about two years out of date, made it look like an ill-formed Christmas tree. The yew's ancient association with churchyards dates from the first Christian missionaries, who preached below the year-round shelter of its spreading canopy, a symbol of everlasting life. Its timber has greater elasticity and strength than any other tree. I hoped people would come and see the yew for themselves. Then I imagined a crowd in the small garden, people touching the needles, children climbing the trunk, and I shuddered.

I had acquired the cutting from the Fortingall Yew, which stands at the geographical heart of Scotland, in a small village not far from Loch Tay. I've never been, but I've looked at many pictures because the yew in the churchyard there is believed to be at least three thousand years old. When English tree surgeons announced they were taking cuttings from the tree to be grown by the Forestry Commission and replanted around the UK, I made the case to the head of Landscape Architecture, who in turn appealed to the Office of the Architect, that if we acquired one we would be continuing the tradition of our revered founders, who planted more than one hundred species of trees on the original campus. The founder argument almost always prevails, and later that year my cutting was planted as part of the Founders Day ceremonies. It was planted in one of the smaller university gardens near the library and dedicated to an employee in Historic Preservation who was retiring, someone I didn't know, but who was deemed, as tradition stipulates, "a person who has made a lasting contribution to the design, planning, and maintenance of the grounds." Fortunately there are no plaques affiliated with these Founders Day trees, just a list kept on the university website, so I know who the yew belongs to.

I met the cutting at the airport and took it immediately to the university greenhouse where I potted it and tended it until planting. By late spring it was well rooted and I hardened it off for three weeks in a cold frame—the first week under a layer of horticultural fleece I special ordered. I prepped the soil in the garden with plenty of chalk before the planting ceremony, and for several winters after that cleared the young branches after every snow. In year seven, I reirrigated the entire garden to improve drainage.

The yew is one of very few conifers that do not bear their seeds in a cone. Instead, each seed is enclosed in a tiny red cup known as an aril, the flesh of which is very sweet and not toxic. It's a favorite of blackbirds. All other parts of the tree, however, are poisonous, so we had to cordon it off behind a low landscape chain and install a sign:

YEW

TAXUS BACCATA

FROM A CUTTING OF THE
FORTINGALL YEW, PERTHSHIRE, SCOTLAND
3,000–5,000 YEARS OLD
PLEASE BE ADVISED: FOLIAGE, BERRY, AND BARK
TOXIC TO HUMANS

It took a long time to settle on the wording. The administration wanted *warning*. I thought something like *please note* would suffice. We compromised on *be advised* and Blake added the *please* at the last minute. Nevertheless, there are complaints every couple of years and I have worried that the tree would be sacrificed to appease the worried mother of a freshman. The poet's prize seemed to secure the yew's future, and for that I was grateful.

The yew stands alone, which is a shame. Many scientists believe trees can befriend each other, intertwining their roots to share resources and bending their branches to make sure each gets enough sun. Some think that a pair can become so close that when one of the trees dies, the other one dies, too. About fifty feet to the west stands a very fine Sitka spruce (*Picea sitchensis*). The weather generally comes from that direction, and as the Sitka tolerates wind blast exceptionally well, I know it creates a shelter belt for the yew. That's something.

And the yew is thriving. In fact, there is something about the yew only Blake and I know, and I caught his eye across the table at lunch. It was our job to care for the trees in that section of the university gardens, including regularly calculating height and girth. The yew is a long-lived species, and slow growing; it usually takes about ten years to reach a height of six feet. My yew was fifteen years old and had already reached twenty. Blake and I didn't know why, but the yew appeared to be growing inexplicably fast.

⸻ Road Trip ⸻

For years my family drove every August to visit my paternal grandmother in New England. We always drove straight through, often packing our own food in a cooler and stopping at a rest area to eat. My father, brother, and I would take our sandwiches to a picnic table. My mother usually stayed in the car. Sometimes I knew why, other times I might have fallen asleep and lost track of what was upsetting her. Everything was dry that late in the season, but the air would be thick with humidity. I would check for spiders, then stretch out on the bench and watch the clouds. In my memory all the colors are exactly the way they are supposed to be: green leaves, blue sky, white clouds; just as a child might draw them. There are no shadings, no unusual effects of lighting or weather.

My father might buy a newspaper, extending our lunch break, which meant he was tired. My mother might smoke a cigarette in the car with the door open, one long leg stretched out onto the pavement, while my brother, clutching some sweet from the vending machine, ran back and forth between them.

After lunch we resumed our positions in the car. My father always drove and I sat behind him. My mother remained in the passenger seat, as always, and my brother sat behind her. The diagonals are what is important here. From my position, I could see the edge of my mother's face, not her full profile unless she turned to tune the radio or look at my father, but enough to gauge her mood. My brother had the same view of my father.

And that is how we grew up, with me watching my mother, my brother watching my father. Of course, the young family in that car is gone, as extinct as any mammal could be. The little blond boy running back and forth with a cookie? His hair turned dark by his teens but he kept running, all the way to California. The father who, later that same summer, brought back a wild cardinal flower (*Lobelia cardinalis*) and tried for years to keep it alive in an inhospitable spot in his too-dry garden? He gave up his wildflower walks. The too-observant ten-year-old? I gave up, too, started paying more attention to books and plants.

Those summer visits were quiet, full of reading and long walks in the woods and almost no socializing. But one night I remember my father shaving and putting on a jacket. My grandmother made deviled eggs and my brother and I were told to dress nicely. I registered these events the way one would a cold snap; strange, but refreshing.

The cocktail party was in a house just down the street and the guest of honor wore a wig and thick beige nylons. She sat in a chair by the window and although she smiled and talked and even had a gin and tonic, she never stood up. Her son, a dark-haired boy of ten or eleven, didn't stray far and brought her a shawl when she complained of a chill. My father had a drink or two more than usual that evening, and I learned from him later that the woman in the wig was dying of cancer. She was dead by September.

The cocktail party had been the dying woman's idea, her last chance to say good-bye to her friends and neighbors. My grandmother was a friend, and she must have insisted we go with her. This was fascinating to me because my family tended to use any excuse *not* to have friends over. Dying would certainly have been at the top of the list.

One memory from those summer drives is particularly vivid. We'd stopped for lunch, as usual, and I was sitting on a bench near a bed of English ivy (*Hedera helix*). A spider had built his web just above the ivy and I decided to toss a little seed pod at him to see how he would take it. The weight of the pod was too much and it tore through his web. He scrambled over to see what had happened. Without any hesitation he clipped the wayward strand, releasing the pod, then set about repairing his home. In no time at all he was back again in the center, waiting, though now at a new angle to the ground.

Driving Lessons

The next time I saw Leo I asked if he was sure he'd been exposed to poison ivy. "My mother thought I was immune to chicken pox until I got it when she was teaching me to drive. I had a terrible case. I missed a week of school."

He described a typical poison ivy rash convincingly, so I nodded.

"Your mother taught you to drive?" he asked, still standing by my table.

"Yes."

"No," he said, smiling.

"What do you mean, no?"

"It's a father's job," he said with mock authority.

"In all other ways my parents had very traditional roles. But my mother was a good driver."

"And your father is not?"

"He's fine, but it meant something more to my mother." She wanted to teach me, for some reason.

The minute I said it I knew it was true, but it was not something I'd realized before.

The year I was fifteen, instead of taking the driver's-education class at my high school, I drove with my mother in the evenings. When I could circle the block without stalling—she insisted I learn on a manual transmission—she let me go farther. We listened to the radio, and she would bring two cans of soda, though I wasn't allowed to open mine until the lesson was finished. I drove while she sipped, marking the beat of songs she liked with a little bounce of her chin.

Toward the end of the semester, my mother and I drove through the hilly parts of campus so I could practice hill starts and I remember her pointing at the Christmas-decorated balconies of the student dorms. "Little rectangles of cheer," she called them. I believe she was happy then. It was the year she turned forty. The next year she helped me buy a used Ford Fiesta, though she had never owned her own car. When that car died, I bought a first-generation Taurus, which still had a manual transmission option. That's Bonnie.

I like to drive but over the years an archive of accidents I've read about, like a mental flip book of tragedy, has stuck in my head. The woman walking to church, hit so hard by a car her head was severed from her body and flew a hundred feet. The teenager on a forest road, impaled by a tree branch, invisible in the dappled summer sunlight, that came through the windshield.

There are others. I've read that the local school crossing guard is not allowed to touch anyone crossing the street, not even the little old ladies who stand on the curb and flutter their elbows like wings for assistance, because if something were to happen, the liability for the city is too great. We hurl ourselves around in cars, but we're not allowed to touch each other crossing the street? It's an absurd arrangement, and by that I mean there are ironies everywhere the world does not allow you to talk about even half as much as you'd like.

I'd stopped eating my burrito. Leo came back and asked if I wanted something else, but I told him I was fine.

The promenade was crowded—Leo had to fit in seven tables to make the venture economically viable—but no one seemed to mind. The McDonald's across the street had hoisted so many American flags from its roof after 9/11 that a good wind made the whole area sound like a marina. Beyond the McDonald's, after perhaps another eighth of a mile of cars, was a larger strip mall called Barracks whose main stores were a Whole Foods, a Bed Bath & Beyond, a Barnes & Noble, a trendy optometrist's, and a Ruby Tuesday. It was by far the more popular mall, doing many times the business of Wayside, which had only El Puerto, a quilting store, and a family-owned pharmacy in that order along the long arm of an L. A salon called Shear Elegance, in which three pairs of flip-flops mounted over a crucifix were the main decor, occupied the corner. Then there was an empty storefront and finally Mrs. Kim's Inconvenience. The Barracks lot was landscaped with mature crepe myrtles that bloomed raspberry red in late summer, purple salvia, boxwood, arborvitae, and seasonal flags. When Barracks filled up, people often parked at Wayside and walked across the road, which was a problem for El Puerto because then people were more likely to eat at the Ruby Tuesday or grab a sandwich at the Barnes & Noble café.

At the table next to mine, two girls bowed their heads to say grace over their red baskets. In the far corner a group of mothers was waiting for their food while a number of babies fussed in car seats around them. Several friends pushed two tables together in the center, but then took out their phones and sat there texting. Suddenly one of them looked up at the speaker system Leo had painstakingly installed, now playing mariachi music. He lifted his arm, cocked his thumb, and pretended to shoot the speaker with his hand.

Leo brought my check.

"What about mosquito bites?" I asked.

"Terrible. They swell up. You?"

"They don't bother me."

He nodded appreciatively.

Silver Linden (*Tilia tomentosa*)

The leaves are shaped like the conventional heart in a deck of cards. The wood has a pale, creamy-brown color and wood-carvers have always preferred it as the best medium for fine wood sculpture. It is also used for hat blocks, shoe lasts, and, because it is very stable, piano keys.

Not a bad choice for my father, but as I got ready for bed it occurred to me that Sustainability Planning would probably object. They were a tough, well-organized department, and there is a widespread belief that the silver linden is toxic to bees. It's not; the truth is, in the late summer and early fall, when the bee's life cycle is coming to an end anyway, there are fewer nectar sources, so they congregate around the silver linden and some number of them die there. But Sustainability would never approve even the appearance of harm to a pollinator.

The Last Whiskey Sour Party

In August my father and I attended a going-away party for the Goulds, an older couple in the neighborhood who were selling the house they'd lived in for thirty-five years. The new owners came, so did dozens of friends and neighbors. The Goulds had raised three children in the place, but when I overheard Beth Gould talking about the move, I couldn't locate the sadness I expected. The house and garden were a bit much now, she said. She and Philip were ready for the next adventure. Someone asked her about the children. Were they sad?

"Oh, they're such homebodies," Beth said. "We travel to them."

The main concern seemed to be renaming the whiskey sour parties for which she and Philip were famous. They planned to serve something different in the new place and hadn't yet decided what it would be.

I recognized faces from the neighborhood and lifted my

cheeks into a smile a few times, but I didn't know anyone well enough to stop and talk. I'm the neighbor they don't know, the one they probably don't like very much, the one they know no better now than the day they moved in. Some of them have asked me for favors: "Bring in the mail while we're away?" "Water the garden?" But I've never asked for a favor in return. Some have tried to be nice about my living at home: "Your roots are here," they say. It's true, they are. Putting down roots is not my problem. I imagine that's what they tell themselves they're doing when the *thump, thump* of cars going fast over the metal plates in the road keeps them up at night.

The Goulds' house was not yet packed for the move, so I wandered through the beautiful rooms. It was an elegant and comfortable home. The furnishings were not too many or too few, the colors were muted and harmonious, the windows were large and clean. It had the feeling of a place that held fine things that were also used and loved. At the doorway to the kitchen, however, I stopped. Here was a different mood entirely. Almost everything that could have a saying or a motto printed on it did: magnets and spoon rests, jars and candles, placemats and mugs, dish towels and needlepoint samplers. It didn't take long to discern the theme:

Friendship is sweet beyond the sweetness of life (St. Augustine)
Friendship is inherently a magnet (Eudora Welty)
Friends are the family we choose (Anonymous)
Happy is the house that shelters a friend (Emerson)
Friends are God's apology for relations (Hugh Kingsmill)

Friends show their love in times of trouble, not in happiness
(Euripides)

Even the Kleenex box by the cookbooks said *Gather friends: Rassembler des amis*. So many centuries of friendship advice, all of it distilled into shades of pastel calligraphy. I wondered if the items had been gifts over the years from devoted friends, or if they were hopeful directives from the Goulds to themselves. Either way, the system had worked, hadn't it? The Goulds' house was full of friends who loved them and wished them well. The Goulds were happy, healthy, and busy. I hadn't even detected irritation in Beth about her children not visiting enough. She'd called them homebodies affectionately.

I refilled my wineglass, which was not (I double-checked) engraved with anything but did have one of those trinkets around the stem that was supposed to help you keep track of your glass at a large party. I wasn't surprised. On the dishwasher I'd seen a magnet that said *Happiness is a friend . . . doing the dishes*.

When I rejoined the party, my father was talking to Beth Gould, his head bowed in concentration, a posture I recognized. It meant he was very interested in whatever she was saying and would not want to be interrupted.

I bumped into Philip Gould by the dining room table. "You're one of the Attaway children," he said.

"Guilty as charged." Small talk is like improv comedy: rarely funny and always one sentence away from fizzling. When I must do it, clichés fill my head like a virus.

He said, "I liked your mother," and my mind went blank.

"Thank you" didn't seem right, but what was? I looked at my feet.

"I remember her teaching you to drive. She borrowed our Volkswagen station wagon to teach you stick shift. I admired that."

I remembered the station wagon, but not that it had belonged to the Goulds. They drove a blue MINI Cooper now, which *I* admired. Their downsizing was consistent and complete.

"Are you looking forward to the move?" I asked.

"Sure," he said. Then he eyed me. "How are you? Are you and your dad ever going to move?"

"Fit as a fiddle" were the words in my head and I was trying very hard not to say them. I was rescued by someone tapping a glass for a toast, and the party began to shift toward the living room.

"Excuse me," Mr. Gould said. "I think I'm needed."

A gift had been arranged by the whole neighborhood (it was the first I'd heard of it), and we watched while Beth and Philip opened it together. The package had been handed to Beth, but she gently insisted Philip open it with her. He did the unwrapping, handing Beth the bow and each piece of paper as he tore it. Then suddenly they were both looking down at a silver plate, reading quietly. They looked up at each other first, both with tears in their eyes. Beth read the engraving out loud, her voice breaking a little bit.

"'Show me your friends and I'll show you your future.'"

Everyone clapped and cheered. All the names of all the families in the neighborhood, many of whom had known the

Goulds for years, were engraved on the plate in a kind of constellation around the quotation (which was unattributed, I noted).

"Attaway" was on there. I checked before I left.

THAT NIGHT I WALKED through the rooms of our house. Unlike the Goulds', nothing in the Attaway home was out in the open; nowhere was anything printed or engraved for all to read. My father had lived eighty years without even wearing a T-shirt with words on it, as far as I knew. And I couldn't remember my mother ever wearing one either. In our house, verses were for memorizing. Books had to be opened, read, searched.

We did have a complete set of *The Oxford English Dictionary,* all twenty volumes. My father gave it to my mother when I was born, a way to remind her that although her circumstances had drastically changed, the language hadn't. It ran across the two lower shelves of the bookcases in our living room. I pulled out volume VI, *Follow—Haswed,* and looked up *friend.* The Goulds' kitchen might have been full of nice phrases and wise ideas about friendship, but they felt like hybrids to me, something cross-pollinated to maximize sweetness. I wanted the original. I wanted to know the first use of the word in English.

And there it was, from *Beowulf:* "*Heorot innan waes freondum afylled.*" (Inside Heorot there was nothing but friendship.) As an English major, I had read the epic in college, but I remembered it only vaguely. I knew my father would have it, so I went to his shelves in the study. I chose the Seamus Heaney translation because it was the most recent and I liked the cover. In the base-ment, my father dropped something in his kitchenette below me, then all was quiet. I opened the book and began to read.

Here is what is relevant to my story: Heorot, the famous palace and mead hall, was built by King Hrothgar as a gather-ing place for his warriors. Grendel, descended from Cain, lives nearby in a swamp with his mother and can't stand the sounds of joy that emanate from the hall. Grendel comes each night off the moors and stands outside to hear how Hrothgar and his men are "settling to it," meaning the wine and the song and the friendship. Eventually the din puts him in such a rage that he breaks down the door and kills most of the warriors. Every night these events are repeated until the hall is abandoned. Then Beowulf arrives and offers to take care of the problem so Hrothgar can use his hall again. Beowulf and his warriors fill Heorot for a rowdy night, then feign sleep. When Grendel ar-rives Beowulf grabs his hand in a mockery of a handshake, and after a long battle he rips Grendel's arm off at the shoulder. The monster retreats to his swamp where he dies. The next night Grendel's mother seeks revenge but is also killed by Beowulf, which is unfortunate. We could use more vengeful monster-mothers in literature.

More briefly: *Beowulf* is a violent epic about the dangers of being friendless. There's a party, the misfit is not invited, he sulks outside, then comes in, wreaks havoc, and is killed.

Quite simply: Without friendship, you become Grendel. Many people don't marry and many don't have children. Some people might not know their mother or father, and a lot of people don't have siblings. But any person who has lived for any length of time has had a friend. Except Grendel, and he became the first monster in English literature.

I looked up and saw the cat staring at me. I asked her what she was expecting. Hester turned to look down the hallway, as if contemplating a reply, then delicately sniffed my big toe and walked away.

Inside Heorot there was nothing but friendship. I wanted that cross-stitched on a sampler for my kitchen. All who read it—well, maybe not *all*—would feel just a little bit doubtful about what was coming for them.

— Accidents —

The last day of August was a Thursday. It had been hot and humid all week, but a thunderstorm that afternoon had done what people always say summer storms do, even though it's rarely true: brought in cooler air. At our dinner at El Puerto, my father said he'd like to walk home.

"What about your car?" I asked.

"I'll get it tomorrow."

"You won't want to," I said. "I'll drive it home for you."

"That's very kind," my father said, handing me his keys.

And that's what I did, but I shouldn't have because I'd had my two beers.

NEIGHBOR SEEMS TO ME a flexible word. You can say "She's my neighbor" and people will think you mean she's your friend.

But if something goes wrong, you can say, "Oh, I don't really know her. She's just my neighbor," and everyone still knows what you mean.

Janine told the police she didn't think I had a drinking problem. "Then again," she said, "I don't really know her. She's just my neighbor."

A witness said the child was "not really all that close" to the car.

In the paper the next day it became "University Gardener in Traffic Accident," but that's misleading because there was no *traffic*. I missed the child and hit the parked silver Lexus of the wealthy college student living in the house her parents bought her. I did this with intention. It was either the Lexus or Mr. Braden's stunning yellow butterfly bush (*Buddleia globosa*) and to me the choice was clear. No other cars were involved and the child was not hurt.

I *was* going too fast, however; that much is true. The two beers on a small dinner were not a good idea, though my blood alcohol level was not over the legal limit. The officer was young and apologetic.

"I have to ticket you, ma'am," he said, grimacing and kneading the back of his neck. "But I don't believe you're a threat."

I thanked him but wasn't convinced. The day before I'd nicked a box turtle with Bonnie's left front tire and sent him spinning into the ditch. I'd seen him with plenty of warning, even among the pine needles dried in masses like pelts all over the roads this time of year. I'm sure I cracked his shell.

THEY SAY TRAGEDIES come in threes, and at the beginning of a surprisingly cool September my father fell in the driveway. I saw him go down as I was going up to bed. I ran outside, where I found him on his back, lucid and calm. Tipped over next to him was a potted cactus, the tall and ungainly night-blooming cereus (*Selenicereus grandiflorus*).

"Please call 911," he said.

"For you or the plant?"

He smiled, I was relieved to see. "Please ask for a quiet ambulance. I don't want to wake the children."

"Are you hurt?"

"I think so. My leg."

"The children?"

"Bella and Henry. Across the street."

"Can I help you?"

"No. It hurts too much. It might be my hip."

I went inside and told the dispatcher my father was eighty years old and stable but there was something wrong with his hip or his leg.

"A quiet ambulance?" she asked.

"I think he means no sirens."

She told me to keep him warm, so after I hung up I took him a blanket. He looked sad as I pulled it over him.

"I don't want you to have to take care of me," he said.

"I don't mind." The words didn't sound convincing, so I knelt down next to him.

He moved his hands in the gravel, clearing little patches with his palms.

I cleared my throat. "Should I ask why you were carrying a night-blooming cereus up the driveway late at night?"

"It's Beth Gould's. She wanted me to have it. The ceiling in their new place is too low."

The *Selenicereus grandiflorus* is sometimes called the Queen of the Night. It blooms once a year and only in the dark, its incredibly fragrant flowers wilting before dawn. In India it's called Brahma Kamalam, named after the Hindu god of creation, and it's thought that the wishes of people who pray to the god while the flower is blooming will be fulfilled. The one my father was carrying was not in bloom.

The ambulance cut the siren before turning down Todd Lane. Still, some of the neighbors came out and stood with folded arms in the blue and red flashing lights. I saw a few children peeking out of windows. As the medics lifted my father into the back, Janine approached, arms across her chest, shoulders hunched against the chill.

"Is there anything we can do?" she asked.

"No, thank you," I said, and must have spoken too harshly because she looked surprised.

"I'd like to be of help," she said.

Of help. To me those words have a geographic sound. Janine Morton, of Help; wife of a medical resident rarely home; mother of Bella and Henry.

"I understand," I said, and managed to add "Thank you" because I am aware of sometimes going too far.

— Rewards —

Not so very long ago, there was almost nothing as touching as a group of first graders crouched in a circle preparing to put in their first herb garden, or vegetable patch, or bed of chrysanthemums. Now there is not much that hasn't been touched by technology and that includes children in the garden. They have all played a video game called Plants vs. Zombies. I've never played it, but I gather players advance by receiving plants with different powers, and so the little ones and even the not-so-little ones—thankfully these school trips age out at about fifth grade—are fond of pretending that the tender shoots they are being given to place in the ground have super-powers. Why photosynthesis doesn't strike them as at least as amazing as killing zombies, I will never understand. I did try that angle.

I also tried competition, if they love games so much, and

divided the class into groups with a promise of prizes to the one that finished its work first. When a parent complained that all the children weren't sent home with a little marigold in a pot, I resigned my school-trip duties. We live in a time when everyone gets a medal and all villains have heartbreaking backstories. No one thinks evil is intrinsic anymore, just someone making a really bad choice.

Blake O'Dell agreed with me, but thought it was a good idea for me to take a break from the school groups. So now, per Blake's instructions, the groups are led by undergraduate volunteers from the Environmental Sciences program. They have boundless energy and seem to relate to the children better, though the first time I observed one of the field trips the undergraduate instructor paused the planting session to send a text. About half the class, fourth graders by my guess, took the opportunity to pull out their own phones, while the rest fell into the blank stare of children long accustomed to being considered less interesting than their caregiver's screen.

Blake O'Dell isn't particularly warm or nice, and he can be bossy when he needs to be—when landscapers mistreat the plants, or high school volunteers fulfilling some academic service requirement work harder on their tans than on the job at hand. But he is never loud, works at what appears to be a slow pace, and yet is so constant and steady, he always accomplishes more than anyone else. Years ago my father told me about walking in the Alps with my mother when they were young. They set ambitious goals and would head out from the mountain hut in the morning at a good clip, leaving the weathered, older crowd of Swiss walkers with their walking sticks far behind. In the afternoon, those walkers always passed them. Always. That was Blake. Of course, it's the old tortoise-and-hare story, but isn't it a little shocking when a myth shows up so clearly in the real world?

Back in July, not long after the poetry prize was announced, Blake had made the case that as the planter and cultivator of such well-remunerated inspiration, I deserved something, too. Apparently the head of Landscape Architecture laughed, but a letter from the vice dean (a mathematician with the heart of a botanist; Blake said he'd often seen him admiring the tree) helped. It took three months to approve and Blake had kept quiet about it the whole time. Then one morning in October he told me that "in recognition of my service to the university and its historical gardens" I was being given one month of paid leave to use as I wanted over the course of the following year.

The story made the paper. In a brief article mainly praising the university's open-minded generosity, the female journalist pointed out that the poetry award had been given to male poets for five consecutive years, so it was nice to see a woman being acknowledged, no matter how tangentially.

Blake, with the melancholy eyes and weather-beaten face, had done this for me. It was more time off than I'd ever had.

Sue called it a minisabbatical.

Leo said it might be life changing.

My father asked if I was going to travel. He was using a single crutch, nursing a bruised hip.

———

THE FIRST THING I did was reread all the posts about Amber Dwight. Several new ones had gone up since I'd last been on the site. The second thing I did was visit the yew. I brought a thermos and a blanket. I picked up a few red and blue plastic cups, no doubt dropped the night before by undergraduates between parties, and worked some fertilizer into the soil around the trunk. Then I sat with the yew and sipped my coffee.

I was being given an enormous gift of time and I wanted to use it well. Fairly quickly I came to three conclusions.

1. I was not interested in finding out who I was alone, which seemed to be the goal of many who explore the power of a year's effort toward something. I knew that person and I was tired of her. I didn't want to take her to Italy, or hike a long trail, climb a mountain, or camp in the woods.

2. I was interested in figuring out who I was with other people, and why that person was hard to be. I remember my mother, not a great keeper of friends herself, used to say, "If you're comfortable with yourself, you'll never be lonely," which didn't feel like the whole story.

3. A trip to the bookstore had suggested my choices were to run to nature (see number 1), disappear into books, or both.

But I was beginning to have another idea. If "Friends are the family we choose," as the adage goes, I was worried I hadn't paid enough attention. Some people, like the Goulds and Amber Dwight, collect friends easily. Others get to midlife, look around—sort of the way you might reexamine your living room when you need a new sofa—and say, What do I have here? What is this room I've made?

Halfway through life, I wasn't sure what I'd made. I finished my coffee, rolled up my blanket, and went home.

I BEGAN LOOKING for models to follow, women's adventure stories, not war making or city founding, but friend gathering and family healing. But all I could find were what I began to think of as the Penelope model. While Odysseus roamed, Penelope stayed put. Her story was psychologically and emotionally challenging—she raised a son and fended off the suitors—but she didn't go anywhere. She stayed in Ithaca and that seems to have set the tone for millennia.

What if Penelope had left? What if instead of waiting upstairs in her rooms, she'd gone to stay with friends in other kingdoms? Trying to find a substitute family when yours is missing is as daring an adventure as any man versus monster. Leaving Ithaca, she might have had an epic in the domestic sphere, pull-out sofas her Scylla and Charybdis, guest rooms her Cyclops's cave. "Wily" Odysseus had to ask his various hosts for a lot of help getting home. Penelope, mindful of manners and, as a woman, trained to please others, would have remembered to ask after her hosts: How are you? How is your home? Do you find you are waiting for something, too? The course of literature might have been very different.

I bought an anthology of writings on friendship and read it straight through. Afterward I was certain of only one thing: friendship is hard to define. Epicurus believed it was necessary for a happy life. Aristotle believed it was necessary for a good life. Cicero thought life wasn't worth living without friends, but that they should be made slowly and cautiously. Montaigne thought friendship occurred once every three hundred years and he was, of course, one of the lucky ones. Oscar Wilde said a friend is one who stabs you in the front, and C. S. Lewis proposed ideograms: if lovers are two people facing each other enraptured by the other's gaze, then friends are two people standing side by side, looking ahead in the same direction.

I suppose today both figures might be looking down at their phones.

In the scientific sphere, friendship is defined as time plus intelligence, and only a few species are capable of it: the higher primates, members of the horse family, elephants, cetaceans, and camelids. For cross-species friendship, three criteria must be met: the bond must be sustained for some period of time, both animals must be engaged, and there must be some sort of accommodation on both sides. So my love for my cat, Hester, who has certainly made no accommodations for me, doesn't count. But the turtle playing ball with the dog, the ape cuddling the kitten? Unquestionably. The internet is full of videos of this sort because humans adore them. And yet how many of us can say we've made an accommodation, a sacrifice seemingly against our very nature, for a friend?

On a walk recently in Duck Woods, I saw two women talking on a corner. They'd been for a run and were warming their hands around cups of coffee.

"You make friends in your twenties and your sixties," one of them said, just as I passed.

I pretended to be curious about something behind me in the road so I could see the other's reaction. She looked down. In my anthology, I'd read that F. Scott Fitzgerald thought it was the thirties and Thoreau was inspired by the forties. The day after his fortieth birthday, Thoreau woke up and made a resolution to celebrate friendship as the centerpiece of his life. "I sometimes awake in the night and think of friendship and its possibilities," he wrote.

But I kept walking. When it felt as if I'd gone far enough, I pantomimed having forgotten something and turned around and headed back.

Now the first woman was saying, "I don't know what I did, Bampf, but I miss you."

The name couldn't have been Bampf, but that is what I heard. Both women were aging well; they might have been in their fifties, but I wasn't sure. My pace must have slowed too obviously because Bampf frowned at me. I had to keep moving, so I don't know how it turned out for them.

My father told me once about friendship, "You have to decide if you're going to take the bad with the good," advice I did not find, then or now, especially helpful. It sounds as if you make that decision once, when in real life it can come up again and again.

— Day Trip —

On a bright October Saturday, I drove to a nearby town known for its Victorian architecture, duck pond, and miniature railway. I packed a sandwich and my thermos and drove the fifty-minute drive in thirty-five minutes. This was a day trip my family made often when I was growing up and I knew the road well.

The day was cold but the shore of the duck pond was crawling with young families. There were six food dispensers around the water, each one with a line of parents helping overbundled toddlers reach for the pellets they were allowed to feed the ducks, one swan family, and a number of geese that probably weren't going to bother flying any farther south because the winters here are warm enough now. The birds were so full they paddled near the center of the pond, seemingly conferring about what to do about the relentless children. The children, some of them trying out Halloween costumes a week early, crept closer and closer to the water's edge, desperate for the birds to eat more. The feeders of birds are always children or the elderly. They are the ones who seem to want that windy feeling of needy birds swirling around, while those of us in midlife crave calm.

The scene was entertaining but not what I'd come to see. I sipped my coffee and wandered toward the railway. Here was an attraction managed by the children themselves because the cars were too small for adults. The parents traditionally crowded the fence near the tiny station where the children boarded and eventually disembarked after a dozen loops of the little oval track. One distraught mother was trying to get on the train with her child, a notably calm boy of about four, but this was not permitted. I could see the conductor in his black-and-white cap shaking his head.

The train whistled and started off, all the parents held up their phones, and all the little children—well, most of them— stared straight ahead, surprisingly stoic. I looked around and there, up the sloped bank, in a bit of sun near a stand of ash trees, was a couple looking toward the train but decidedly re- moved from the rest of the parents. This is what I'd hoped to see. The woman smiled and waved; the man stood with his hands in his pockets. Impossible to tell which child was theirs, but my question is this: Was that child any less adored because mother and father stood so far back from the rest of the crowd? All the rest of the parents were jostling to record all twelve, tired loops. The parents on the slope took no pictures at all but had a good view.

I unwrapped my sandwich. As the ride finished and I watched one little girl in a white hat with a pom-pom disembark and look around on tiptoes until she spotted the couple on the hill, I felt a cramp in my stomach. The train whistle blew for the next ride and her parents waved down to her. The little girl dodged the next surge of parents to get up the hill to her own.

Are they an unhappy family? Where's your evidence? Her mother hugged her when she climbed up the hill. Her father gave her a snack. But it does teach you something. You grow up thinking it's natural for the ones who love you most to keep their distance. Love stands apart; love lets you come to it. This isn't wrong, exactly, but I wanted to learn how to stand closer.

⸺ Peeps ⸺

The week after my trip to the duck pond, I invited Sue to meet me at a restaurant for dinner. I told her I'd started thinking about using my leave to visit old friends.

One thing that is a bit annoying about Sue is that what she is thinking plays out across her face.

"You have peeps?" she said.

"I don't call them that, but yes. Why do you look so surprised?"

"You've never mentioned them. Where do they live?"

"I haven't?"

"Not once that I can remember. How long have we known each other? Ten years?"

"I'm not for everyone, I know that. But I do have some friends."

"But you don't talk about them. I've never even heard their names."

"I can tell you their names."

Sue smiled. "That's not the point. Friends don't have to be like seedlings placed at intervals along a border. It's okay if they overlap."

I decided to change tack. "You're good at friendship," I said.

"It's my religion," Sue said, and I nodded, for I had given her the opening. She was serene, pleased. I had the feeling she'd been waiting a long time to say these words in just this way.

"What else is there?" she asked.

"I don't know. It's not easy."

"Why not?"

I sighed. Having begun this conversation, I nevertheless did not know where I wanted it to go.

"Making or keeping?" she asked. "Which do you mean?"

"All of it," I said. "It takes a lot of time."

She smiled again, and what her smile said was, What is time in the face of friendship?

"You were an only child," I countered, holding her gaze. I just now saw the importance of this. "I think friendship is easier for only children. It makes sense. You needed friends more."

She raised an eyebrow at me. "And are you close to your brother?" she asked.

We each took a sip of wine, eyeing each other over the rims of our glasses.

"We're not good at staying in touch," I admitted. "But my whole family is like that. I have a couple of aunts and uncles and a few cousins, but we don't gather. We don't have reunions."

"Well, a lot of families don't have reunions."

"We don't celebrate milestones."

"None of them?"

"Nothing." Growing up, I knew people who always seemed to have family arriving for one reason or another: birthdays, Thanksgiving, the Jewish holidays. I remember my mother saying, "Centuries of persecution will do that to a people." We were Episcopalian.

"Maria thinks you're afraid of being vulnerable," Sue said, setting her glass down with exaggerated care. Maria was Sue's partner. "I told her you've never seen May prune a climbing rose."

"Maybe," I said. "But now I'm thinking about visiting friends, putting myself at their mercy. Maybe I'll stay a fortnight." I was thinking of Austen and her heroines. It was always the most vulnerable, the orphaned and unmarried, who went visiting.

"You're kidding."

"I've always liked the idea of them. Why not?"

"I think the fortnight is dead, along with calling cards and letters of introduction," Sue said.

"No one has guest rooms or servants anymore, either. I'm sure that's part of it."

She wasn't listening to me. "This is a bad idea," she said, shaking her head. "I hope you don't mind. I think it's the responsibility of good friends to be very honest and sometimes say hard things."

"No, it's okay," I said, mostly thinking I was glad Sue considered us good friends. Then she told me a long story about a time when she'd stayed too long with a friend of hers.

Some people are good at telling stories about themselves. I know this is called sharing and it's considered a virtue, but generally when I try to talk about myself the stories come out fast and abbreviated. I don't know the word for this. Repressed, probably. But couldn't it just as well be modest? "We gloss," my father once said about the Attaways, which seemed about right.

Sue's visit was a disaster and the friendship was never the same. She finished by saying, "And a fortnight is *two* weeks."

"I know. I won't. I guess I'm just thinking of a time when that's what friendship was. Instead of texts and coffee dates, people stayed with one another, for a fortnight if needed. Can you imagine? Having friends who would take you in for that long. Fortnight friends."

Sue looked doubtful, but we shared a dessert, and she offered to feed Hester and bring in my mail whenever and for however long I went away.

"Thank you," I said. I hesitated, but then decided to tell her I'd thought of a name for her company, the one she'd dreamed about that brought streams through living rooms.

She was surprised. "You did?"

"Riverkeeper."

Sue raised her eyebrows. "I like it."

AFTER DINNER WITH SUE, I started noticing pairs of friends everywhere. On an unseasonably warm day in November, I ate my lunch downtown and watched two old men, one tall, one short, taking a constitutional around the perimeter of the square in front of the courthouse. They walked quickly and looked like they'd been friends for a long time, or at least they'd figured out how to perfectly match their strides, which couldn't have been easy given their height differential.

A few days later I was getting coffee at a café and noticed two women sitting in a corner, deep in conversation. They were older, and one was tall and heavy, the other short and thin. I don't know why the universe was sending such fairy-tale-like pairs my way; I'm just recording what I saw. I must have been staring because as the young barista passed me my coffee, she said, "Aren't they so cute? They come in every day."

"Every day?" I said.

"Seriously. Every day. I mean, I talk to my BFF all the time, but we can't have coffee. She lives in Maine."

"That's too bad," I said.

"Oh, that's okay. We Skype every day."

I tried to think of something I could say I did every single day. The only thing that seemed absolutely true was brushing my teeth.

MY NEXT EL PUERTO NIGHT, a Monday, Leo ate dinner with me.

"Do you mind?" he asked, one hand on the back of the chair, the other holding his plate. I was inside because the promenade was closed up for the winter season, the tables and chairs stored behind the restaurant. He'd already brought my order and was wearing a nice shirt and no apron.

"Of course not." I sat up straighter.

"How's your father?" he asked.

I told him his hip was still sore, but the doctor didn't think anything was wrong.

We ate quietly for a little while, then Leo said he was thinking about landscaping the promenade in the spring, maybe with a green border built somehow between the counter and the parking lot. He wanted to know what I thought.

"With containers?" I asked.

"Could be. I don't have any definite ideas. I was hoping you might."

I looked out the window at the space. I said I had a few books on container gardening he could borrow.

After a minute he said he'd also been thinking about putting some flowers around the garage.

I set my silverware down, wiped my mouth, and told him annuals grow well in hanging baskets, but he should be careful about viruses, which are incurable, and overwatering, a common mistake. A lot of people get started with containers and have no idea. The plants get mildew or aphids or white spots and it's all an eyesore before you know it.

"Okay," he said. He looked discouraged, but I was just being realistic.

I told him my burrito was particularly good.

He smiled. "I'm glad. I made it for you."

"You're not working tonight."

"I made an exception for you."

"Oh." This surprised me. "Thank you."

"You're welcome."

HE'D MADE A DESSERT, too, but I didn't stay. I needed to walk.

My mother, a city girl who often despaired at the lack of anything to hang a walk on in Anneville, invented something she called the redeemable element game. On every street you try to find something redeemable, not in the sense of cashable, but in the sense of finding the one thing in your field of vision that either soothes or keeps you moving. I play it when I'm agitated.

My mother and I had the pink Cadillac always parked in the same spot on the hill near the university; the mysterious corner where we always smelled cigarette smoke, though we never saw anyone smoking; the long garden where someone grew corn and zinnias in alternating rows; the patch of pink phlox under the railroad bridge by the Econo Lodge; and the wine bar downtown where, if you sat with your back to the door, you could pretend you were somewhere other than Anneville. It was a desperate game, I see that now, but it worked for her for a while.

It was the wine bar—new ownership several times over but still a wine bar—I found myself standing outside after I left El Puerto. It had grown dark enough that the group of friends at the inside front table saw only their reflections in the window when they looked out, not me standing on the other side of the glass. They weren't that much younger than me, maybe mid-thirties. There were eight of them, men and women, and they were celebrating something, because the waiter was pouring champagne. Four of the friends sat along a bench with their backs to me, two sat at the ends of the table, and two were on the far side facing me. Their phones were out, but while I watched not one was touched. The waiter seemed to know the group, or liked them, because he was smiling and talking to them. What was not to like? To a person they looked happy and comfortable, so comfortable, with one another. While I watched, several of them wrapped an arm around the person next to him or her in what looked like a spontaneous act of affection and friendship.

It started to rain, but still I stood there. I watched them order their food. That took a long time, but the waiter never lost his patience. One of them got up from the table and I worried she might be coming outside to smoke so I scuttled to the side, but she walked toward the back of the restaurant. When she returned, she leaned over to sit back down on the bench, her face coming within inches of mine on the other side of the glass, but she didn't notice me.

For a little while, one of the women talked and the whole table listened. It must have been a sad or poignant story because two of the other women wiped their eyes. But there were smiles, too, and laughter at the end. Then the appetizers arrived and the whole table was talking again.

After the appetizers I left abruptly, walking faster and faster in the rain. I thought about all I'd read. They say friendship alleviates physical health problems and increases our level of happiness. They say that spending time with friends can lower blood pressure, decrease depression and stress, and help relieve chronic pain. One study showed it has as large a positive effect on health as quitting smoking. In another, researchers took a group of students to the base of a steep hill and fitted them with heavy backpacks before sending them up the slope. Some walked next to friends, while others walked alone, and the students who walked with friends gave lower estimates of the weight of the pack. The longer the friends had known each other, the lighter they reported the backpack to be.

Yet spending time with friends is the first thing we drop when life gets busy. This has been shown, too. Exercise is good for our health, and even the lazy might exercise a couple of times a year. Many people now eat kale. Who among us makes plans to visit friends regularly? We heed so much radical health advice, why not this?

"Do you have somewhere you can go?" I heard someone ask a homeless woman as I walked.

"*Who is near?*" Siri asked me when I fumbled with my phone.

Grendel was alone, but Dante had Virgil and Odysseus had his men and gray-eyed Athena. A man on a quest always gets a crew or a guide.

I passed the cemetery, where it had become popular to place little solar lights by the gravestones. There were probably two dozen soft blue lights glowing in the rain. I pressed something on my phone and ended up with Siri again, her words floating up from the dark.

"What can I help you with?

"Here are some of the things I can answer.

"Who is near?"

I turned the phone off. I wanted to answer that question myself. We document our lives for people near and far with status updates and photographs, but we rarely just show up.

I decided to show up.

"Poor May's going on a trip," I whispered, and vowed to buy a new suitcase in the morning.

Crack Willow (*Salix fragilis*)

The crack willow grows well along watersides and takes its name from a feature of its twigs. If you pull one back with a quick tug, it breaks away from the larger stem with an audible *crack*. Nobody is sure why the tree grows such brittle twigs (it is also sometimes called brittle willow), but the property aids its general propagation. When twigs are torn off by gusty winds, they are carried downstream and take root easily on damp banks. Crack willow is, in other respects, a typical member of the willow genus, *Salix*.

This might have been my father's attempt at a joke after his fall. The leaves are bright green and the catkins in early spring are lovely, but there is no obvious waterside on campus and the tree is highly susceptible to snow and ice damage.

Or it was his way of asking me to stay home. He hadn't cracked a bone when he fell, but he was worried about the next time.

Crack willow (*Salix fragilis*)

II

The day I bought Grendel there was a sparrow in the Walmart. I spent awhile choosing my suitcase, but I spent longer watching the sparrow's small black beak tilting this way and that, questioning the high white ceiling full of fluorescent lights. The front doors had an air lock, which would have been hard for a bird to navigate, so I assumed he must have come in from the garden center, a dismal area adjacent to the parking lot with only the most average evergreen shrubs and seasonal chrysanthemums (genus *Dendranthema*) in three colors: too yellow, rusty orange, and bad purple. Mounds of forced hardy mums plunked along curbs and into garden beds this time of year are my least favorite tradition of the season. I'm not a fan of using annuals in landscaping in general, and to use a hardy mum, which is a perennial, as an annual is an affront. Chrysanthemums were first cultivated in China as far back as the fifteenth century, and, along with the plum blossom, the orchid, and bamboo, it was considered one of the Four Noble Plants. Now the mum is to flowers as the Red Delicious is to apples; a ubiquitous fraud. The mums outside Walmart were arranged in long, single-color lines on aluminum bleachers facing the parking lot, their fall from grace complete. The only thing worse might be the grocery store orchid.

A young employee mistook my staring for interest. "Can I help you find something?" she asked. She was wearing gardening gloves and holding a trowel, but it wasn't clear that she'd been planting. She was very clean.

"Oh, no, thank you," I said.

"Hard to choose, isn't it?" She looked at the mums with me. "They're all so pretty. I did yellow and purple this year."

Back inside, the sparrow wasn't hard to find. He was making quick trips from the air space above Pet Supplies to Bedding and back, which seemed like a sound plan. Anyone in Pet Supplies would be sympathetic to his plight, but when I walked over there the section was empty. I stood beneath him for a while. The archway to the garden center was large but low, and he didn't seem to be aware of it. I stood next to the dog food projecting flight lines. It seemed possible for him to fly out that way, but he looked confused by the lights and perhaps the Christmas music.

A woman about my age turned into the aisle and stood before the cat food. Her cart had several giant boxes of Goldfish, a dozen rolls of wrapping paper, and now the tins of cat food she was layering in.

"There's a sparrow," I said, pointing at the ceiling.

"Excuse me?" she said.

"There's a sparrow up there. I think he's trapped."

She frowned and looked up. The little beak opened and we heard a few pitiful chirps.

"That's too bad," she said. "Did you tell someone?"

"No. Should we?"

"Oh," she said, resuming her work with the cat food, "I've got to get home."

"Right. I mean I could."

She counted her tins, then looked back up at the sparrow. "I'm sure it happens all the time," she said, beginning to push her cart out of the aisle.

"But does that make it better?" I said.

She laughed as if I'd made a joke and kept going.

In the Home Goods section it took me nearly twenty-five minutes to settle on the American Tourister Meridian 360, which was advertised as "a functional travel companion for all your fun adventures." The bag featured a multidirectional wheel system that promised to allow me to "push, pull or turn in any direction with effortless mobility." Hardly the help of the gods, but it wouldn't hurt. There were several black and navy blue models, but I decided on the slate gray before realizing there was only one left in that color and it was damaged. It had a black scuff mark like a sash across the front and one of the outside zippers was bent. "We take our friends as we find them, not as we would make them," Samuel Johnson wrote. I took the banged-up suitcase—and hoped I might get a discount at the register.

The sparrow was still chirping as I navigated back to the front of the store, but I didn't look up.

I wanted to ask someone if birds flew into the store frequently, but my cashier was the yellow-and-purple-mum girl from the garden center.

"No mums?" she said, genuinely perplexed, when she saw me.

"No," I said. I knew I should follow this with some nicety, but I couldn't think of anything. "Not today," I offered as cheerfully as I could.

She smiled and I decided to leave it at that. I didn't ask for a discount.

— Invitations —

There's a difference between showing up and showing up without an invitation. I was not willing to do the latter. And it was not as if I needed to make a list of friends I might visit and then narrow it down. I don't have that many friends, and by that I mean I knew who I wanted to see.

1. Lindy Ascoli. Hers was the house I spent the most time in growing up, her phone number still as familiar to me as my own. She has always been serious, yet smiles readily, and seems to genuinely enjoy being a stay-at-home parent to three girls.

2. Vanessa Meyers. Lindy and I met Vanessa in eighth grade. She was taller than both of us and had beautiful dark hair and eyes and a sense of fun more daring than mine or Lindy's. The three of us became a close trio,

though eventually Lindy and Vanessa became closer than I was to either of them. Lindy went to Connecticut for college, married a few years later, and has been making a home there ever since. Vanessa has lived in six different places in three different countries, recently married a divorced man, and became a stepmother to twin boys. In all the pictures I've seen of her lately, she is leaning to touch her head against someone—a friend, one of the stepsons—as if anchoring herself.

3. Neera Khadem is a college friend. My roommate was a disappointment, as I'm sure I was to her, and I was soon spending more time with Neera, whom I met in an introductory psychology class. A driven woman from the West Coast, she stayed up late and dated a lot. I did neither. Nevertheless, she's my closest tie to a time in my life I remember fondly. I met her husband, Adam, before she did. I introduced them, so we have that bond, too.

4. Rose Gregory chose me. She scanned the list of graduate student names and decided we should be friends, a May and a Rose in a Landscape Architecture program. She's assertive like that. She's a few years younger, having come straight to the program after college, and yet focused and calm. I'm not sure what I offered her, but even after I left the program and she finished and moved back to England, she stayed in touch with me.

Lindy, Vanessa, Neera, and Rose. Through some mysterious combination of shared experience and common interest, they seem to feel something for me and I for them. There are other friends I found and lost, friends I had for a little while but couldn't keep hold of. As a child I was, if anything, an overeager maker of friends. There is a picture of me at a swimming hole when I was nine, one arm tight around the shoulders of another girl, the other arm blurry because I am waving it up and down, joyous at having made a new friend. The word *befriend* is related to *bind* and I was clearly trying to bind her to me. That friendship didn't stick, though. I can't even remember her name.

Lindy, Vanessa, Neera, and Rose. I have strong images associated with each, a combination of memories and social media posts, I suppose: Lindy walking confidently across the park, bouncing on her toes to appear taller. Vanessa writing from New York about the family she's making. Neera in Seattle buying a pot of begonias for her desk before sitting down to work. Rose walking in Clapham Common, her navy pea coat buttoned up neat and trim to go grocery shopping. These images have meaning for me, they feel like clues toward something, and I try to keep them in mind.

It's usually not appropriate to invite yourself to anything. The one exception seems to be when you are in a town where a friend lives. You can say you'll be in town and many times this leads to an invitation to stay. Some people will announce to a large group that they will be around on a certain date and will be at such and such a place on a given night and hope friends will join them. This scattershot approach feels foolhardy to me. Unless you are certain you are very popular, I'd rather apply the Kitty Genovese lesson to seeing friends and pinpoint one at a time.

"I wanted to pay you a visit," I said on the phone. Why do we "pay" visits and "receive" guests? It's the language of accounting, of ledgers and balance sheets. But no one likes to admit keeping track, good manners forbid it.

"You *wanted* to?"

"I do. I still do." I'm not good on the phone.

"Really? I'd love that. When were you thinking?"

"I'm flexible. I have a lot of time off work."

"Is everything okay?"

"Yes. It's sort of a reward."

"A reward? Like a vacation?"

"Sort of. It's complicated."

"Well, anytime, May. It would be great to see you."

I looked at my calendar. "What about in two weeks?"

"Oh, soon. That's great."

"It could be later." I flipped calendar pages.

"No, that's fine. I'm just surprised. But we're in town, it's no problem. Are you thinking a weekend?"

"Maybe four or five days?"

"Okay. Are you sure everything's all right, May? How's your dad?"

"He's fine."

"Can you leave him that long?"

"He's very independent."

"That's good. Are you still living—"

"Yes, still in the house."

"Well, I can't wait to see you. It's just sort of sudden and . . . not really like you."

"I'm aware of that."

"You are?"

"Yes."

"Okay."

". . ."

"So how much time are you taking off work?"

"Four weeks. The university is giving me paid leave because someone won a lot of money for a poem about a tree I planted."

"That's so cool! Congratulations, May."

"Thanks. But, please, don't think you have to entertain me at all. That's not why I'm coming."

"Great, we'll just hang out and catch up. Thanks for reaching out."

Is that what I was doing? Reaching out? It sounded desperate. The phrase made me picture someone walking blindfolded. I'm certain Amber Dwight would have managed with more flair, but I did the best I could.

— Packing —

A *trip* is a journey or an excursion, but it can also be a stumble or misstep. To avoid the latter, I bought a copy of Emily Post's *Etiquette*, which confirmed my strengths as a guest:

I am quiet and don't have any food allergies.

I'm not a heavy or light sleeper, an early or late riser.

I don't get cold easily.

I am not good at "curling up." I've never been comfortable putting my feet on another person's sofa.

I like wine and you never have to make me decaf.

I don't need ice cream, fudge, taffy, or a T-shirt to feel like I've been somewhere.

I take a professional interest in botanical gardens and arboretums, obviously, but that doesn't mean I must see them everywhere I go. They're not always as good as people think they are.

I enjoy seeing a good river, but I've never climbed an observation tower that wasn't a waste of time.

I like zoos and aquariums in the presence of a child, but small museums make me nervous.

My friends had all referred to "catching up" and I wanted to do that, probably while "curling up," but I wondered, is that when you ask the questions you can only ask the people who have known you longest? When do you say, What do you remember? What was I like? Was I nice? I hate the word *nice*, but it's the first thing that comes to mind. It seems to me that your oldest friends can offer a glimpse of who you were from a time before you had a sense of yourself and that's what I'm after. When do you say, I know you probably have better friends, but my father is old, my brother is absent, and I need to know who is near.

What I packed: two pairs of jeans, one dress, more shoes than I'd probably need, several tank tops, cardigans, and scarves (because layering is to travel as tuning is to music), the Emily Post, the usual underthings and toiletries, a flashlight, and a thermos.

— Departure —

Just as there is no explaining why some people can't board by their assigned row, there is no explaining how Grendel fit into the measuring bin at the gate. I had hurried there after my standoff with the child at the water fountain and now the flight attendant, who a moment before had been certain Grendel was too large, snapped the stretchy string of the claim ticket in her hands.

"That's impossible," she said.

I was surprised, too, but I pulled Grendel up and out and smiled apologetically, which seemed to annoy her more. She crushed the tag in her fist and turned her attention with a fresh smile to the next person in line. I spun Grendel around to roll in front of me, the position he seemed to like best, and headed down the ramp.

I see a lot of nice airplane-window shots on Instagram, but to me the idea of being pinned against the curved metal wall of an airplane by a stranger or two is intolerable. I am devoted to the aisle seat. I keep a scarf with me for holding over my nose against other people's aromatic food, and I hold a book in my hand as I board the plane. I do not take any chances, and a chance would be leaving a window of opportunity open in the time it takes to get a book out of my bag.

Something about travel makes people confessional. Why isn't it enough to be going with friends to celebrate your fiftieth birthday in Las Vegas with matching T-shirts? Why does your seatmate need to know all about it, how long you've planned, how crazy your boss thinks you are? Maybe everyone just feels raw and vulnerable in their flip-flops, another mystery. To me, bare feet and travel go together as well as spiders and cuisine.

I turn the reading light on before fastening my seat belt.

In the end the plane was overbooked. No one volunteered to be bumped, so they held a lottery and I lost. I had to close my book, wrestle Grendel from the overhead bin, and deplane. The attendant who had measured Grendel seemed to be suppressing a smile.

I would arrive on the Thursday and leave on the Monday. That's how Lindy and I had described the visit, setting it up by phone, the definite articles giving the days a certain dignity. Now I'd be arriving on the Friday. I called Lindy, who seemed unfazed by the change.

"I'm just sorry for you," she said. "Travel delays are the worst."

But as I went to treat myself to a Bloody Mary, I didn't feel irritated. I felt relieved. Lindy and I shared a lot of history. The thought of some quiet hours in a hotel room before the burden of arrival sounded good to me.

The televisions behind the bar were showing sports and violence, and people talking about sports and violence. The night before, while I had finished packing and gone to bed, another black man had been shot by a white person in uniform. I had not seen this news yet. Coverage of a football game was on two screens, this story was on the other two.

The television anchors were reporting that a group of young men had been running around Central Station. It was either a game or, possibly, parkour, reports hadn't been confirmed, but two of the group claimed to be parkour instructors who sometimes performed in public spaces. When they were finished one of the men approached a window to buy a train ticket. He slipped his backpack off his shoulder and dropped it to the ground, then leaned over to get out his wallet. He was out of sight of the ticket window for five or six seconds. When he stood back up, the clerk shot him in the chest with a gun she kept in her purse. He was thirty. The woman, fifty-six, said she was scared *he* was getting out a gun. She'd noticed him running around the station that evening.

I signaled to the bartender to cancel the mixer in my drink and watched the screens closely, trying to follow along through the misspellings and broken rhythms of the closed-captioning.

Suddenly a man a few stools down said loudly, "Oh, man. Don't do that." He was black and shaking his head. "You don't need to buy me a drink."

The white man next to him pushed back his stool and stood up. "I just wanted to do something nice for someone today and you were sitting right here." Both men wore blazers and jeans.

The bartender waited as if in stop-motion, holding aloft a credit card and turning to the first man who had spoken.

"I'll get the tip," the black man said, and the bartender swiveled back into motion.

The white man nodded, signed his receipt, and left.

Gradually the restaurant din came back up, most tables likely debating whether the gesture was a weak attempt at token solidarity or a genuine desire to make a connection. Just recently I'd read about a fever of kindness running through a small Southern town in which the residents started paying the bill of the car behind them at a McDonald's drive-through. For several days, cars paid for each other in an unbroken line.

My visiting plan included three white, one brown (Neera is half Iranian), and no black women. I regretted this imbalance and wished it were otherwise. I'd had a chance. A girl named Danielle Belieu arrived in mid-September the year I was in fifth grade, and perhaps because her apartment building and my house were close, Danielle wanted to play often. I remember a snowstorm when we both came out of our homes and played in the middle of the street. I can see her standing under a streetlamp with the snow coming down fast. We already knew school would be canceled the next day and we were happy. Danielle had a big smile, with upper teeth that were going to need to be straightened. My braces were already on. When she wanted to play, I often said I had to do homework, which was sometimes true and sometimes not. She was the only person I knew who lived in an apartment building. She was also the only black girl in the fifth grade.

The next year we chose instruments in school. I wanted to play the cello, but Danielle chose it so I didn't. Instead I chose the viola, a miserable instrument on which I achieved nothing. Danielle eventually won a music scholarship to college.

The first year I was on Facebook I found her and sent her a message. She responded, I wrote back, and I never heard from her again. Sometimes the door to friendship doesn't open as far as you think it might, and you're vulnerable standing there on the threshold, not yet in or out. It was uncomfortable online, and Danielle had endured the feeling in real life. I wish I could say the school where Danielle and I met is more diverse now, but it's not.

I looked back at the TV screens. Now there was a report about people wearing backpacks across their chests as a symbol of solidarity with the slain man, the way they had once put up their hoodies. The closed-captioning was badly delayed, but one commentator seemed to be suggesting a backpack worn in front was better for your posture anyway. Two birds, one stone, or something like that.

THE AIRPORT HOTEL'S specialty was freshly baked cookies any time of the day or night. NEVER HAVE TOO MUCH ON YOUR PLATE FOR A COOKIE! was the lengthy slogan, printed on a sign near a huge plate in the lobby. A white employee of the hotel was eating them, and when the clerk helping me noticed him, he winked at her and made an appreciative growl. The clerk, a black woman, shook her head. "I see you stealing my cookies," she said. She repeated this sentence several times, the emphasis moving around: "I *see* you stealing my cookies; I see you *stealing* my cookies." The man ate at least five more.

I lingered over some brochures, and when the man finally left, the clerk rolled her eyes and replaced the cookies.

— Arrival —

M any wise things have been said about a visit's proper
length.

It was a delightful visit—perfect, in being much too short.
   (Jane Austen)
Fish and visitors stink in three days. (Benjamin Franklin)

And we know that Hans Christian Andersen ruined his
friendship with Charles Dickens by staying with him three
weeks longer than planned.

The arrival, however, has been overlooked. Welcoming a
friend into your life is like folding egg whites: it should be done
gently and with good technique, leaving lots of air. Enthusiasm
has its place—exclamations, hugs, compliments—but mainly
the trick is to make people feel comfortable right away, and to
do this both guest and host must conceal any work that has

gone into the convergence. The preparation of the house, the altering of schedules, the travel. It's usually a mistake to launch into a story about the difficulty of your travels, though that wasn't always the case. In the *Odyssey*, it was part of the accepted pattern of hospitality:

The guest arrives.

The guest is offered a bath and/or fresh clothes.

The guest is given food and drink, usually at a feast.

The guest is questioned about his travels; there are speeches on both sides.

Everyone retires for the night to a soft bed.

Today people will leave a key so the guest can let herself in. Some want to be there when you arrive. Others want to meet you at the airport. Some show you where you'll sleep right away. Others ask if you'd like something to eat or drink. The eating schedule is almost always the first hurdle for a variety of reasons: you may or may not have eaten at the airport, dinner may be early if there are children involved, or late if work is an issue. There are almost never feasts and entertainment, at least not the first night. And if there are, you are definitely expected to talk during them, though Odysseus got to eat first and talk afterward, which would be my preference. Almost no one asks if you'd like to bathe.

Speech making is out of fashion, but questions do arise. A common one: "How's your family?"

Ah.

A Venn diagram might be helpful here. In the Attaway family Venn diagram, if x = my father, y = me, and z = my brother, then the point of greatest overlap between x, y, and z is where we agree that my mother died. What caused her death, relevant details of her last few years, her state of mind when she died, remain in dispute. My father and brother agree she was bedridden. My brother and I agree that her bedridden state was at least partially voluntary. My father and I agree her lack of mobility contributed to her death. My brother believes it was an accident. My father blames himself, while I have wondered what it is fair to ask of loved ones. Can we ask them to take care of themselves for our sake, because we love them, or is that an inherently selfish request?

Or perhaps a parable would be better. A woman was going from her forties to her fifties when she fell into a depression. It stripped her of her energy and beat her down. A man happened to be going down the same road, and when he saw the woman, he had good personal boundaries established and so passed by on the other side. So, too, a woman; when she came to the place, she spoke to the depressed woman but grew frustrated, and was also very busy with her own life, and soon passed by on the other side. But a Samaritan, as he traveled, came to where the woman was; and when he saw her, he went to the woman and bandaged her wounds, pouring on oil and other balms. Then he put the woman on his own donkey, took her to an inn, and took care of her. The next day he took out two silver coins and gave them to the innkeeper. "Look after her," he said, "and when I return, I will reimburse you for any extra expense you may have."

Which of these three do you think was a neighbor to the woman? The Bible says the one who had mercy on her. But what is mercy if, as in my mother's case, the woman wanted to be left alone? What happens if the woman never again leaves the inn?

On a message board about the original biblical story, I found this question: "Which of the following could be reasonably understood as an accurate biblical definition of the term 'neighbor'?"

1. Only one's immediate associates.
2. Only one's extended social or religious group.
3. Neighboring nations and cultures.
4. One's enemies.
5. All humanity.

The most popular answer was 2. How can we live in a time when social media makes us *friends* with people all over the world, but our sense of *neighbor* is shrinking?

So, how's your family?

I could say we've grown more comfortable with peace than joy, patience over hope, and perseverance feels the same as love.

I could say happy families are supposed to be all alike, but even the happiest, after forty years, probably has some reckoning to do.

I could say my brother hasn't been home in eight years.

But I don't. How can I when I've just arrived? Most of us, especially women, don't have the luxury of an Odysseus or a Beowulf to deliver an epic speech upon arrival. So I say we're hanging in there. And, where should I put my bag?

House Proud

I knew Lindy's house would be thoroughly decorated; I followed her on Instagram. I used to marvel at her acquisitions, impressed by the early finesse of her home. She had real furniture at a time when most of us were still working with futons. When every room was decorated to its full potential, she started designing napkins and placemats and curtains. She'd recently posted a picture of a pink tape measure and a stub of pencil on a windowsill. No caption, but the ethos it conveyed was unmistakable. Her DIY impulse was boundless, extending even to the surname she and her husband shared. They combined pieces of their last names to make an entirely new one: Lindy Ascoli (English) and Max Casaubon (French) became Lindy and Max Casacoli, suggesting an Italian heritage neither of them had, though their kitchen was painted a beautiful Tuscan yellow.

Lindy picked me up at the airport with her middle daughter, Mona. I saw them standing by their car outside baggage claim, but I waited until Lindy saw me. I think she might have done the same thing. It's worth remembering that Odysseus always arrived in disguise, which is a lot easier than showing up as yourself. In the end, Lindy and I seemed to see each other at the same moment, then hurried toward each other, smiling. We hugged and laughed, said it had been too long, and immediately started trying to remember when we last saw each other.

"No school today," Lindy said, putting her arm around Mona. "Max is at home with Jessie and the baby."

"She's grumpy," Mona offered.

"The baby?" I asked.

"No, Jessie," Lindy said. "It's okay. It doesn't matter."

"She's a preteen," Mona explained. I nodded. I knew a lot about what that meant from Lindy's Facebook posts. I also realized I knew a lot about Mona—she liked ballet, she was good at math, she'd gotten her first-grade class to start composting—though I hadn't seen her since she was a baby. This didn't make me feel confident, though. I felt like a spy who had read a dossier and wasn't sure what I could reveal.

"Do you know your multiplication tables?" I asked.

I'd overstepped the mark. Mona looked up at her mom.

"She's getting there," Lindy said. "One through four, right?"

Lindy's face looked older, which meant mine did, too. I think she was thinking the same thing. We said almost simultaneously, "You look great," and gave each other a new and tighter hug, Lindy up on tiptoe.

"Oh, it is good to see you," she said. She sounded a little relieved.

———————

MANY MIGHT HAVE BEEN daunted by a visit so near Christmas, but not Lindy. She'd said on the phone she was organized "this year," but I know she is organized every year. I've seen the pictures. And indeed, when we arrived at the house, it was thoroughly ready for the season: candles in the windows and lights on the bushes; two trees up and decorated, one in the living room and one in the den; mantel and windows draped in evergreen boughs.

"I haven't done the village yet," Lindy said.

"The village?"

"The Christmas village. I've been collecting pieces for years."

I gave them their presents in the foyer. My timing was off, gifts should come later, but we were gathered awkwardly around the front door, where Lindy's husband, Max, and their elderly dog had greeted us next to a full-scale gingerbread house. Max and I seemed about to resume the how-long-has-it-been debate, so I opened Grendel and got out the gifts. I had books for the girls and a set of hand towels with an embroidered strawberry (Lindy's side of the long ago Dairy Queen debate) for Lindy. She remembered and laughed, then showed me to the guest room so I could get settled.

Emily Post had very high standards for guest rooms and thought every hostess should be obliged to spend twenty-four hours now and then in her own to better understand its strengths and deficiencies. Is the lighting adequate? Are there enough blankets? She even insisted on a shelf of good books. Post would have been mortified by the common, modern-day inter-pretation of a guest room as storage space, stuffed with old ex-ercise equipment and off-season clothing, maybe an inflatable mattress and a rolling desk chair bumping around. Lindy's guest room was somewhere in the middle: no books and the walls were bare, but there was a real bed, a good lamp, and plenty of blankets. I also had my own tabletop Christmas tree decorated with tiny red balls and baby candy canes. Next to it was a little framed quote: *The ornament of a house is the friends who frequent it* (no attribution). It still had the price tag on the back and I couldn't help wondering if Lindy had just acquired it.

"Your guest room is lovely," I called in the direction of the kitchen.

"Oh, thanks," she called back. "It's a work in progress."

There's always something nice to say about someone's home—the light through the front windows, the color of the kitchen—and it is important to find that thing and say it.

After lunch and the baby's nap, Lindy, the children, and I drove to a place where there was a boardwalk along the ocean. It is a rule of visiting, I think, that the things that make real estate valuable also make an outing pleasant: a water view, ele-vation, and local attractions, with the water view being perhaps the most popular. A museum or historic village? Not everyone will share your interest. A bike ride? Not everyone will have the energy. A drive or a walk can be nice, if there's something to see, such as a mountain or waterfall. And it is always a good idea to have a place in mind for a snack. This is why the English have tea, the Germans have the *Kuchenstunde* (cake hour), and

Americans eat too much ice cream. No one *needs* to eat between three and four o'clock in the afternoon, but it is a pleasure. It is also the best way to extend good cheer until cocktail hour.

We followed the boardwalk along the rocky coast and at the end there was an observation tower. It was mild for a December day in Connecticut, but windy, which made conversation difficult. We were constantly brushing the hair out of our eyes, or turning an ear out of the wind to hear each other better. Lindy asked if I was going to see Vanessa during my travels. I said yes but we hadn't settled on dates yet.

"I'll be curious what you think," she said.

The wind blew the hair across her face and I couldn't read her.

"About what?" I asked. But she didn't hear me, or didn't answer, I couldn't tell which.

We climbed up the tower (all of us except the preteen), agreed that, yes, we could see even farther, then climbed down and followed the boardwalk back to the parking lot. We were almost to the car when Mona raced to the top of a nearby hill, so we went up after her (all of us except the preteen). Elevation was the theme of the day, it seemed. I practiced my winter tree identification while Mona ran in circles. People are surprisingly impressed when you can point to a bare tree and say, "Common lime." Or, "Ginkgo." The second is particularly easy because when leafless the branches look like model train tracks against the sky.

On the way home we stopped for ice cream.

— Catching Up —

Saturday morning Max took Mona and the preteen to ballet so Lindy and I could have some time alone. I had been about to take a shower, but instead we lingered over coffee in the kitchen while the baby played in a bouncy seat. Lindy couldn't quite believe I wasn't traveling for another reason.

"You don't have a work conference?"

"No."

"Is there a garden you need to see?"

"No."

"This is just . . . vacation."

"Yes, kind of. I'm trying to pay more attention to my friends."

Lindy glanced around her kitchen. It was cozy and warm and in need of a good sweeping, which she probably knew. Her gaze fell on a large bouquet of juniper and birch branches I'd already seen on Instagram, where a week ago it had had a sepia filter. In front of us now, something felt decidedly lost, but what exactly? Should I mention I'd seen it on Instagram?

I pointed at the arrangement. "That was so pretty," I said.

Lindy shrugged. "Do you want something to eat?" she asked, an edge to her voice.

I remembered something I'd read about May Sarton, who looked forward to her friends' visits with singular intensity. On one occasion, when a friend made a comment about some wilted flowers, Sarton became furious and spoke so harshly—screamed—that she lost her voice. Her inner life was in turmoil and she had a great need for the spaces of her life to be seen and appreciated. If any crack in the façade was noticed, her anger rose quickly.

"No, I'm fine," I said.

"I almost planned a party," Lindy said.

"What?"

"For you. And the holidays. I'd love for you to meet some of my friends up here, and for them to meet you. But"—she looked down at the baby, who had started to fuss—"I just couldn't pull it off."

"I'm so glad you didn't." The extent of my relief must have alarmed her.

"Are you okay?"

"Oh, I'm fine. Fit as a fiddle. I just came to see you." The thought of the almost-thrown party had me desperate not to waste any more time. I gestured at the pot of honey on the table.

"You know what I should have brought you? A honey pot with the proverb 'Yet there is a friend that sticketh closer than a brother.'"

Lindy looked confused.

"You know. Gift shops sell all kinds of stuff—spoon rests and dish towels—with sayings on them."

"I know."

"So that would be funny. Because honey is sticky?"

She shook her head. "That is so you," she said. Affectionately, I thought.

"I mean it," I said. "You're my oldest friend. I've known you longer than anyone else."

Lindy leaned forward and gently bounced the baby. "It has been a really long time."

"You were always so happy."

"Was I?" She shook her head in disbelief and I knew why. Her mother had been drinking too much when we met, though we didn't understand that at the time.

"What do you remember about me?" I asked.

"Oh, I don't know. The way you did your hair. Your ponytail had to be perfectly smooth, remember? No bumps. And you were so neat. Remember how you would blow on your notebooks to get all the eraser dust off?"

The baby fell asleep and Lindy sat back in her chair. She looked at me intently, then, in a voice that was a notch or two quieter, said, "I used to leave at night and drive around."

"What?"

"I'd find a parking lot, usually that one at the mall, you know, close to the interstate. I'd park and just sit there, listening to the highway."

"Was it safe?"

"Probably not. There was that movie theater, so people would come out from late shows. I don't know. I just sat there. I thought I was going crazy," Lindy said. "My father acted like everything was normal, so I didn't know what was real." She poured more coffee for us. "I feel like we should be drinking wine, but that would be ironic."

"We were so good," I said, after a minute.

She knew what I meant. Vanessa had been more fun, more wild. Anchored by her stable parents, she seemed to have the necessary leeway Lindy and I did not.

"Poor Vanessa," Lindy said.

"Why? Isn't she happy?"

"It's a lot all at once, you know? Marriage, twin boys. A dog. Have you met Richard yet?"

"No." They'd gotten married at a courthouse, with only a small celebration for family afterward.

"Well." Lindy seemed at a loss for words. "It's true I don't know him well yet, but we had a picnic in Central Park with them recently and she was trying so hard. Taking care of Richard, playing with the kids. She was tireless, but didn't seem quite herself." Lindy sighed. "She'll be fine, she always is. She has her mom. You know they talk every day?"

We shook our heads, both of us trying to imagine what that would be like. Then we saw Max turn into the driveway with the girls. We pressed our cheeks and wiped our eyes. "We'll talk more tonight," she said.

I nodded and prepared myself for the family's full presence in the kitchen. Sometimes as a guest it's hard to know where to be. "Would now be a good time to take a shower?" I asked.

AFTER LUNCH WE WENT TO a bookstore so Mona could use a gift card she'd won at school. Lindy bought some Christmas presents and we waited while they were gift wrapped.

"I used to do all my own wrapping," she said sadly.

On the way home, we stopped for a snack at a café in a barn. There were several farm cats roaming about and a deck with a view of fields. The blended scent of coffee and manure was strange, but Lindy settled at a table to nurse the baby. Just as that was done, Mona spilled her juice, so I held the baby while she took Mona to the bathroom. When they got back to the table, the baby's diaper needed to be changed, so we wordlessly switched children and Lindy went back inside again. It was exhausting.

I felt some pressure to make conversation with Mona, so I asked her if she wanted anything else.

"No, thank you," she said.

I looked at the clouds, which were of many shapes and shadings that afternoon. I told Mona that a cloud has to be 150 feet thick before it blocks the sun.

"Why?" she said.

"That's just how much cloud it takes."

"Cloudy days are warmer than sunny ones," she said.

"Yes, that's sometimes true."

"My mom says it's always true."

"Oh, okay. Well warm air rises and the clouds probably keep it locked in."

"Why?" she said.

I sighed. "Because they're mean."

Lindy reemerged with a sleepy baby and settled her into the stroller. We still had some coffee in our mugs, so she relaxed into her seat with a sigh. Then Mona said she was cold and wanted to go home.

In the car Lindy apologized, but I told her not to. The best way to travel is to surrender a little bit of your personality, and I was enjoying not being the most difficult one.

ODYSSEUS MIGHT HAVE HAD to make speeches and outwit gods, but no less difficult is having to wait out the children to have time with your host. That night, when the children were finally in bed and the wine was poured, Lindy and I had a chance to resume our talk. We'd been looking forward to it all day, but now that the time had come, we were both tired. Lindy admitted to being so tired and overwhelmed lately that she'd started outsourcing everything: landscaping, housecleaning, carpooling, cooking. "There just isn't enough time," she said. She was unwrapping the Christmas village as she spoke.

"But you can't outsource friends," I said. I'd meant it as a joke, but it came out sounding melancholy.

"True," she said, unwrapping a porcelain rural skating pond.

"You're in charge of a lot," I said.

Next she unwrapped the two little magnetic figures that spun wildly around the frosted-mirror ice when she wound the key on the bottom. She set the whole thing down on the coffee table and we watched it together for a moment.

"I, on the other hand, sometimes get home from work and don't know what to do with myself," I said.

"Oh, May. Really?"

I hadn't meant to talk about the challenge of living alone, so turned my attention to landscaping, since she'd brought it up. I told Lindy it felt like everyone now aspired to outsourcing their yard work. It was happening in Duck Woods, too. Then I told her about a yard I loved in which the owner, in an effort to ward off deer from her rhododendrons, had tied perfumed strips of white cloth to every plant.

"It's ghostly at night, but it's also kind of beautiful. It shows how much she cares. Poetry only exists in a garden if it's tended by the people who live there." Suddenly I remembered Lindy's manicured lawn and that she was one of the outsourcers.

"Did you say ghostly or ghastly?" Lindy said. She smiled, and we both sipped our wine. I remembered that when she moved into the house years ago she'd ripped out a whole bank of wild hydrangea (*Hydrangea arborescens*).

Now Lindy unwrapped a little snow-covered drugstore and put it on the table next to the pond. "You know," she said, "when we were little, you were the one who was more into decorating your room. Remember?"

I did.

"I'd come over to your house and you'd have a new poster or you'd have rearranged the furniture or something. And it was always so neat and perfect. I shared a room with my sister and couldn't change anything without her consent. I was so jealous."

"And now you're the one who's mastered the art," I said.

She unwrapped a glittery carousel. Next came a tiny train station.

I thought I was ready for bed, but I surprised myself. The light was dim and Lindy was burning an impressive number of votive candles placed strategically around the room. I don't know if it was the late hour, the flickering light, or the fairy tale quality of the village being unwrapped, but I found myself sharing more than I usually do.

"You know, after my mom stopped getting out of bed," I said, "I'd clean my room at night. And I turned my bed around so that I was facing the window when I fell asleep. Do you remember that?"

"I do. I didn't know it meant anything."

"I thought if I could keep my eyes on the trees and the sky something magical would happen."

Lindy shook her head. "All this stuff going on and then we'd get together and study for algebra."

"I wonder why I brought that up," I said, staring at the very polished floor as if I might read the answer there.

"You don't need to have a reason," Lindy said. She finished her wine and set down her glass. "Wait here. I need to give you something." She left the room and came back holding a small white box.

"What is it?" I asked.

"Open it."

Inside on a bed of cotton was a deer, a little fawn, made of glass. It had long spindly legs that were ridiculously fragile. One of them was broken and had been inexpertly mended with glue.

"I wanted my room to be more like yours," Lindy said. "This was going to be the start of my own collection, but I never got any more."

"You took it?" I'd had a collection of these glass animals when I was little and the deer had been my favorite.

"I put it in my pocket when I was at your house. That's how the leg broke."

"I can't believe you never told me."

"I'm sorry."

"Oh, it's okay. I mean, you could have told me. I don't think I would have been that mad."

"Your whole house was so cozy compared to mine."

"Really? That's not how I remember it."

"Your mom made dinner and lit candles every night."

"Your mom went shopping with you and hemmed all your pants."

These things were true, and neither of us knew what they'd meant at the time. Our sad mothers, doing their best.

"But Vanessa's house," Lindy said.

She meant that of the three homes, Vanessa's had been our

favorite. Her mother often invited us for school-night dinners and weekend sleepovers, things that were impossible at our houses. Her father took piano lessons and her mother played tennis. They seemed to be working on themselves still, which was not the mode of our parents. Eventually Vanessa had parties when her parents were out of town, and even unattended, Vanessa's home somehow felt the most secure.

"Whenever I tried to invite someone over for dinner," Lindy said, "my mother would say, 'We don't have enough.' What does that even mean? We had enough food."

"It means it was too hard for her."

"I fly to the grocery store if one of the girls wants to have a friend over. Last week I got a speeding ticket going to get ground turkey for one more burger."

We were too tired to laugh or cry. We hugged, then Lindy turned to straighten the living room before bed. Each of my friends has a distinguishing trait or gesture that I sometimes don't identify until I see it in a stranger. Then a flash of something—the reaching for a hug on tiptoe, Neera's steady walk, the way Vanessa presses her lips together and Rose stuffs her hands in her pockets—will remind me of my friend and I'll wonder why I hadn't noticed it before.

Watching Lindy's back as she leaned over to fluff the sofa cushions where we'd been sitting, and straighten the Christmas village pieces on the coffee table, then work her way around the room to blow out each of the votive candles, I wondered what it felt like to work so hard on a home. She'd told me earlier that she matched the liquid hand soaps in the bathrooms to the color of the walls. She was thrilled when a brand she liked introduced a French lavender because it solved the problem of the upstairs bath.

In the guest room, I tried to put the fawn on the bedside table, but the mended leg was longer than the others and it couldn't stand. I settled it on its side and turned off the light.

That night I dreamed I lured someone or something out of the house on Todd Lane and we fought on a hilly slope that doesn't exist in Duck Woods. We fought for a long time, until finally I tore off his arm (without any blood or gore), and he was on the ground, crying, "All I did was grow up."

Walking Distance

S ometime in her forties, my mother stopped moving forward. Somehow when we weren't looking, she must have curtsied, performed a little shuffle sidestep, and exited stage right. In retrospect, she'd been rehearsing for some time. She went up to bed often without saying good night, or stayed home from family outings with ambiguous symptoms.

"You'll be fine without me," she always said.

She grew up in New York City and told stories about a magical New York childhood: Rockefeller Center and the big tree at Christmas, skating and picnicking in Central Park. After college she rented a tiny studio and walked to her job at a magazine every morning. She was beautiful, with large dark eyes, a quick smile, and quiet manners. She met my father one afternoon on a park bench where she was eating her lunch and he was reading. She left New York to follow him to graduate school.

She was away from the city for a long time, and when she

finally went back she took me. I was sixteen, she was forty. I held her hand and we walked everywhere. When I got tired, I asked if we could take a bus or the subway, but she said New York was a walking city. Everything was walking distance, she said, so I squeezed her hand and tried to keep up.

My mother always said she knew my name before I was born, before she was pregnant, before she was even married. She'd always known, she said, that one day she would have a daughter named May.

"What if I'd been a boy?" I would ask.

"I knew you weren't," she said.

"You didn't have *any* boys' names picked out?"

"I knew you were a girl," she said simply. "I knew you were my May."

May. May may help. May, help? I was the plan all along, but it wasn't enough. I was born into a role I couldn't play.

The first Christmas she was in her room, I gave my mother a pot of reindeer moss (*Cladonia rangiferina*) wrapped in some silver foil. It's a remarkable little gray-green lichen that can survive just about anything. Keep it in the dark, freeze it, dry it to a crisp; it just goes dormant and waits for things to improve. Eventually my mother had a line of them on her windowsill. After she died I threw them all out, but for all I know they're thriving in a landfill somewhere. I don't care for it as a Christmas decoration anymore.

Sometimes I think my mother slowly removed herself from the story until the story simply no longer had a role for her to play. But now I'm forty and what do I know? We had happy times, though our happiness was always a little desperate because it was never an adequate fix for whatever was making her sad. That is how grief infects families and turns some of us into detectives. The first grief was my mother's; I inherited it.

My first winter break home from college, I called my mom from a phone booth in the town square (this was when there still was a phone booth in the town square). She had been in bed all day and I thought it would make her happy to know I was looking at the city tree all lit up for Christmas. She'd always loved it.

A fabulously beautiful woman was waiting to use the phone. Her long winter coat looked like rabbit fur and her hands were tucked into a muff. She looked like a princess, as if she'd just dismounted from a sleigh. I turned toward the phone box and hunched over the receiver.

I asked my mom if she'd thought about volunteering, perhaps with children or animals? There was a long pause, during which I could hear her sniffling.

I peeked out at the waiting lady. A handsome man was talking to her, offering her the use of his cell phone.

My mother asked if the tree was pretty.

Yes, I said. It's beautiful. Do you want me to come get you?

Maybe, she said.

But I knew she didn't. We'd been here before. She wanted to come, until she didn't.

Local Attractions

Sunday morning, Mona knocked on my door very early. I called "Come in" before I was fully awake. I couldn't remember where I was, which bed, which house, and it took a minute for the room to right itself.

"My mom says you're sad because you're too old to have children."

I turned my head and blinked. Mona stood in the doorway, stroking her Hello Barbie's hair. She'd shown me the day before how the doll was programmed to have conversations. Blessedly, she was quiet at the moment.

"She told you that?" I said, struggling to sit up.

"She told my dad, but I heard her."

I smoothed my hair. "Well, you know, your mom was a really good babysitter when we were growing up."

"So?"

"I wasn't."

"You were a bad babysitter?"

"No, I didn't babysit at all. I hated it."

Mona's eyes widened, then she turned and left.

IN THE AFTERNOON, Lindy and I went for a drive. She took me to the town's historic center where there is a whale fountain. Just the tail, actually, rising up out of the concrete like a dropped ice cream cone with flippers. Lindy said in summer a stream of water dribbles off the flippers and parents sit on the steps all around while children splash. We were across the street from the train station; to the left was a street corner with a couple of boutiques featuring loose women's clothing and leather bags. The idea had been to walk around the waterfront a bit, but the wind had come up and the shops were mostly closed. I watched a toddler in a harness veer close to the whale tail, but the leash in his mother's hand went taut before he could touch it.

"I don't love this town, actually," Lindy said. "But the schools are good and Max's work is here. So."

It was uncharacteristic of her, this confession of present unhappiness, and I wasn't sure how to respond.

"But you seem so settled. Your house and garden."

"Sometimes I drive around and pretend I'm a tourist in the area, just to make things interesting." She laughed at herself. "What about you? Are you happy in Anneville? You could go anywhere."

"That's what I'm trying to figure out."

I asked if there were any more café-barns I needed to see.

Lindy rolled her eyes and said she'd take me to a place I'd really like.

"How do you know?"

"Just wait," she said.

The Coffee Greenery smelled of roasting coffee beans and there were plants everywhere in "living" walls, which I'd seen before, and in "living" sofas, which were new to me. Many were ferns, which was not surprising. Ferns are highly adaptable and grow in almost every habitat on earth. More impressive were the soft mosses and other lichens that were growing in pouches along the tops of the sofa cushions. You could lean your head back and feel like Titania in her bower. A sign on the wall informed customers about improved air quality and oxygen levels, but I knew that already. We sat on one backed with Irish moss (*Sagina subulata*), its little white flowers in bloom, and I couldn't stop smiling.

"I could live here," I said.

"You are too nice," Lindy replied.

"No, really."

"I'll have to put some moss in my guest room."

I asked if she'd heard of May disease. She shook her head.

"It's when all the worker bees in a hive leave all of a sudden . . ."

"Sorry," Lindy said. She had bumped her drink and some of it spilled. "Let me just get some napkins." She stood up, ran into someone she knew, chatted briefly, got the napkins, and returned.

"Sorry," she said. "Go ahead."

I tried to relocate my enthusiasm for the conversation. "The bees abandon the hive sometimes. Except the queen, who is left behind. No one knows why or where they go."

"And it's really called May disease?"

I nodded.

Lindy stirred her cappuccino. "Wow. So what are you saying?"

Two women behind us were talking, one of them energetically describing a recent trip until the other said, some impatience in her voice, "Yeah, I saw all this on Facebook."

The friend stopped talking. "Oh, right," she said.

Here's a question: If a friend tries to make conversation out of a social media post you've already seen, do you let her? Consider it, because new material can be awkward.

THAT NIGHT, I found Mona's Hello Barbie in my bed, tucked in next to my pillow. When I pulled back the covers, she spoke to me.

"Yay, you're here!" she said. "This is so exciting. What's your name?"

"May," I said, against my better judgment.

"Fantastic," Barbie said. "I just know we're going to be great friends."

I wondered if I needed to cover her head to turn her off. "How do you know?" I said.

"I can just tell that you're a nice person," Barbie said thoughtfully.

I was silent.

"You're welcome," Barbie said happily. "How are you feeling today?"

"Oh," I started, thinking I'd tell her the day was over, but something in my tone tipped her off.

"I'm sorry to hear that."

I looked out the curtains. They were made out of a gauzy material that filtered the sunlight nicely during the day but provided questionable privacy at night. I'd put on my nightgown in the closet. Now that it was dark in the room, I could see the trees moving in a wind I couldn't hear. At home my windows rattled in their frames.

"Do you want to play a game?" Barbie asked.

"Really?" I said.

"What do you want to do when you grow up?"

"I don't know," I said, mimicking what I thought was a typical girl's response.

"What about a veterinarian?" Barbie said.

"Animals don't like me."

"I'm sorry to hear that."

I thought we might be done, but Barbie continued.

"What about a scuba-diving instructor?"

"I am a botanist," I said firmly.

"That sounds amazing!"

I shifted in the bed, ready to grab Barbie and turn her off, but the movement somehow redirected her questioning.

"Hey, can I get your advice on something?" she asked. She explained that she and her friend Mona had argued and weren't speaking. "I really miss her, but I don't know what to say to her. What should I do?"

"I don't know," I said.

"You're right. I should apologize!" Barbie sounded so relieved. "I'm not mad anymore. I just want to be friends."

I grabbed her. There was a tiny button on the minuscule waist. I pressed it and waited, half afraid I'd activated another mode, but she was quiet. I held her under the bedside lamp to get a better look. Lindy had said these dolls were very popular, built from scratch by the best engineers in Silicon Valley to be the perfect friend. The more I stared at her, the more I thought she looked like someone remembering to smile, not someone who was actually smiling.

Souvenir

Emily Post has pages and pages of directions for hosts. About being a guest she writes, "The perfect guest not only tries to wear becoming clothes but tries to put on an equally becoming mental attitude." So, which is harder, hosting or visiting? It depends on what kind of person you are, I suppose. Perhaps I'm neither. Walking through the airport I felt like a sailor on land after a voyage, glad to have firm ground beneath my feet again.

When I reached my gate, I realized I'd left my phone charger at Lindy's house. I wheeled Grendel back into the concourse until I saw a tiny airport store where I could get a new one. The woman behind the counter was wearing a sari and every time she had to come around the counter to help a customer, she dipped and elegantly swept the fabric to the side. I purchased what I thought I needed, but when I got back to the gate and plugged my phone in, it didn't work. Grendel and I rolled back to the shop, dodging excited kids, steely business-men, and a team of young women in giant sweatshirts.

The Indian woman was helping another customer. I thought I wouldn't bother her, so I stepped around the counter to get another charger. She came rushing over.

"Oh, no, no," she said. "Please. Let me help you."

I explained the problem and she shook her head. "It will work," she said. "It will work."

I said it hadn't and that I needed a different charger.

"No, that is the one."

"But when I plug this one in the charging light doesn't turn green," I said. I tried stepping around the counter again so I could reach the one I thought I needed.

"No, no. Please," she said. "You are not allowed to come behind the counter."

I stepped back and as I did so I saw a sign that said merchan-dise could not be returned once opened. She could have pointed out the sign and been done with it, but she hadn't.

"I will get in trouble," she said, looking up and down the concourse as if her boss might appear. She took out her phone. She spoke quickly for a few minutes in Hindi, all the while watching the concourse. When she hung up, she said, "My son says this is the one. Sometimes if your phone is"—she made a flat-line gesture with her hands—"it takes time." She plugged my phone in behind the counter. "Leave it. You will see."

I had my doubts, but I waited. She rang up a few other customers, and several minutes later the green light on my phone appeared.

UNPACKING IS EASIER THAN PACKING. When I got home I took out of Grendel the jeans; the dress I'd never worn; the tank tops, cardigans, and scarves; the shoes, toiletries, and underthings; Emily Post; my thermos; and a pink tape measure. I'd lost my flashlight and the pink tape measure was not mine, but sometimes what you pack and what you own are not the same. Aren't we all magpies, more or less? Borrowing from our friends' lives as fast as we can, gathering what we need to live?

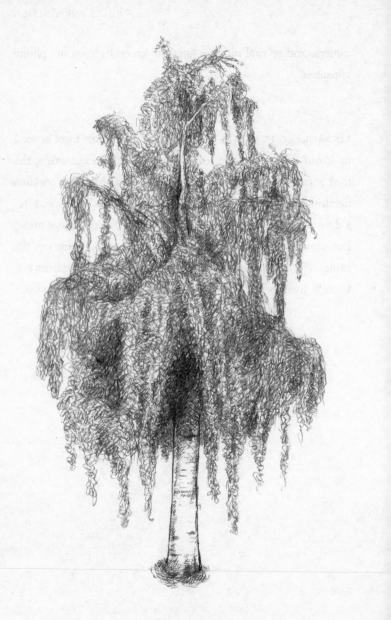

Weeping birch (*Betula pendula*)

III

Weeping Birch (*Betula pendula*)

If the weeping birch sounds like a depressing choice for a memorial tree, then you are not familiar with its twig structure. It can grow fifty to one hundred feet tall with a crown of slender, weeping twigs at the end of each branch. The effect, particularly in winter when the leaves are down, is of a firework just at the moment the sparks turn to cascade to the ground.

The tendril-like branches of the weeping birch allow plenty of sunlight to reach the ground beneath it. Thus it is common for a wide variety of mosses, grasses, and flowering plants to thrive in a birch forest. The tree is considered a "pioneer," a hardy species that is the first to colonize a previously disrupted or damaged ecosystem, beginning a chain of ecological succession that leads to a more diverse, steady-state ecosystem. In other words, it's a nurturing tree that doesn't want to repeat the mistakes of the past.

This tree sheet was taped to my side door when I got home from Lindy's, and judging from its condition, it had been up a few days and endured a rainstorm or two.

I don't know why people start thank-you notes with the word *just*. Just a quick note to thank you for a wonderful time. Just wanted to say thanks for everything. It reduces expectations right from the start. It says: I understand the importance of saying thank you, but I won't be writing a real letter. It says: I'd like to follow the best social conventions, but I won't be spending that much time on it. I've even seen stationery that has "Just a Note" printed on the front. If you start there, why write the note at all? Consider the synonyms: *merely, barely*. Would you write: Barely a note to thank you for the visit? Merely a hasty paragraph to acknowledge all you did for me?

When I wrote to Lindy, I used my best stationery, creamy white, by which I mean if a tree is going to be made into paper, the paper should be high quality. I also sent her a pot of butter-yellow daffodils. Cut flowers make me sad, so I send potted ones if I can. This way Lindy's landscaper will have the bulbs to plant in her garden when the flowers finish.

Certainly thank-you notes don't require thank-you notes;

that would be a never-ending hell. So it was odd to see a reply of sorts a few days later on Lindy's Facebook page. A photograph showed my card propped against the potted daffodils. The vase of juniper and birch was gone.

> Feeling blessed. Just spent a long weekend with one
> of my oldest friends. Best tonic in the world!

It's true *tonic* can mean refreshing, but it also means bracing. It seemed to me it had been both. Part of the trouble with friendship in the age of documentation is that Lindy knew I would see her update, so it was a communication to me. But it was also a communication to the rest of her friends on Facebook. In a few words, she had summarized and packaged our visit for broader consumption. Nothing wrong with that these days, but I don't always understand the rules.

What would it mean if I didn't comment, or post my own picture and reflection? In just one minute scrolling through the rest of my feed, I found myself wondering: Is my dining room table that pretty? Do I miss my cat that much when I'm away? Am I cool enough to dance to eighties music and bake banana bread at the same time?

I liked Lindy's post and left it at that. Only connect, after all.

MY FIRST DAY back at work, Sue asked me if I was on Twitter much. We were covering the topiary on the president's lawn to protect it from winter snow.

"No," I said.

Sue stood up and raked her bangs across her forehead from left to right, a habit of hers that often resulted in dirt on her face when she was gardening. "So you haven't seen."

"Seen what?"

Sue explained that while I had been visiting Lindy, the reporter who'd covered the original grant—her name was Abby Mara—had tried to reach me. When she couldn't, she'd talked to Sue instead.

"I'm sorry, May. I think she must be a frustrated poet or something. She is just so interested in you having this leave."

"What did she want to know?"

"She caught me at the end of the day. I was so tired. Blake and I had spent the afternoon raking the Green." I knew what that meant. It was one of the hardest jobs of late autumn. On the rest of campus, leaf blowers could be used, but the Green, a large, terraced lawn at the historic center of the university, had to be raked by hand. Allegedly this was in keeping with the traditions of the founders of the university; mainly the faculty who lived in cottages around the Green preferred it because it was quieter. Every year Sue grumbled, and I agreed with her. Living on a college campus should not feel like living on an estate with a grounds crew.

"She wanted to know if you were traveling. Where were you going? Were you taking all the time at once or in bits and pieces?"

"Oh, that's okay."

"I ended up telling her about the fortnight idea."

"But I'm not doing that."

"I know. But that fortnight-friends thing you talked about."
She raked her bangs again, leaving a smudge above one eyebrow.

"Yes?"

"Well, she loved it. She wrote another story about you that appeared in the online version of the paper."

"Really?"

"Yes. And it went viral."

"Viral?"

"Pretty viral. She started a hashtag: fortnightfriend."

"But I've never used a hashtag in my life."

Sue looked confused. "That doesn't matter."

"But it feels weird."

"Hashtags always feel weird."

I pointed at my forehead to indicate the smudge on hers.

"Well, this one doesn't seem so bad. I'm sure it won't last."
Sue stripped off a gardening glove and rubbed at her forehead with the back of her hand. "But check out your Twitter feed when you get home, okay?"

I had two thousand new followers that night. Abby Mara might have invented the hashtag, but she credited me with the idea and had linked to my account. Two days later, the hashtag—and, interestingly, its plural—were trending:

> Hugs to all my #fortnightfriends!
> You know who you are.

> #fortnightfriend visit this weekend! Hooray!

Work on your #fortnightfriends y'all. Mine
saved my life.

Thrilled to have a #fortnightfriend from each
place I've lived. #lucky

It must have been the time of year: mid-December, visits
with family and New Year's resolutions looming. The collec-
tive consciousness of Twitter was primed to embrace friendship
as a balm for a challenging season. Distinctions were debated:
the fortnight friend could not be someone whom you *wanted* to
visit for two weeks, but someone who *would have you* for two
weeks. Some said it wasn't real—no one had visited like that
since the Victorian era. Others pointed out how little of modern
friendship is actually real (IRL).

The backlash started the following week:

Asked my boss if I could have time to visit my
#fortnightfriends. Yeah right. #mustbenice

Can't I just be your #friend? #fortnightfriend

Srsly thought #fortnightfriend was a
euphemism for something else.

What the #@&% is a fortnight?
#fortnightfriend

Eventually Lindy posted on Facebook again.

> When I met May Attaway in sixth grade I was the new
> student in class and we didn't immediately become
> friends. She was quiet and didn't seem too worried
> about people liking her, which was cool but intimidat-
> ing. That year we had to write stories every week for
> our teacher, who would give us a prompt. May and I
> always got 99% on them, week after week, because our
> teacher said he never gave a perfect score. But then
> one week May got 100% and he asked her to read it
> to the class. I remember sitting there thinking, I've got
> to be friends with this girl. One of the best decisions
> I've ever made. May is my original #**fortnightfriend**.
> So proud of her!

There was no photo; the daffodils must have wilted. I liked the post and thought about leaving the blushing emoji, but I have never used an emoji and I didn't want to start. I also didn't want to craft a comment that would be a further testament to our friendship for the benefit of others. The story she mentioned had been about a cat at a shelter who is not adopted and is ulti- mately put to sleep. It felt like the only good way to share that would have been to make a joke about it and I didn't want to.

THE SEASON WORE ON. We dutifully put up the signs around campus that said THIS LAWN CLOSED FOR WINTER REST AND

RECOVERY, which the students always ignore. Christmas came and went. My father and I had dinner together, but otherwise didn't make much of a fuss. Holidays are hard for the same reason social media is hard: they allow us to think we know what everyone else is doing. My father and I aren't great at doing things at the same time as other people: planting on the last frost date, reading the latest bestseller, eating turkey. I don't know if it's chronic procrastination or a dislike of team sports. Back in the era when we still gave each other thoughtful Christmas presents, we used to have a tree and put up stockings. We don't have a tree now because I can't stand all the nice things said to the fresh trees each year as they're brought inside, decorated, and loved, only to be unceremoniously dumped on the curb a few weeks later, and my father can't stand the artificial ones. The town mulches the trees for the park service, but it still makes me sad. If I were a six-foot Douglas or Fraser fir, I'd be very bitter.

Then it was my birthday, the last day of the year. I've never been able to get used to it. Long ago my mother would say that on New Year's Eve the whole world was celebrating my birthday, but that just made it worse. When it became clear I would have been far better suited to a quiet day buried in the middle of the year and shared with no one else, she gave up. I am grateful, however, I was not born in May, and I assume, although I have never asked, that my parents would have chosen a different name had I been. Possibly not; the Hebrew meaning of my name is "wished for" child, which my mother knew. It's also, and this I prefer, another name for the hawthorn flower.

Unfortunately, the December birth flower is the narcissus (common name daffodil), specifically the winter-blooming variety, or the paperwhite. I have spent many a birthday sneezing from the strong scent of these surprisingly durable flowers. My father always gives me a pot of them that he buys at the grocery store wrapped in green or red foil. Daffodils were brought to Britain by the Romans, who thought the sap had healing powers. In fact, it contains crystals that irritate the skin.

American holly is the lesser known flower for people with a December birthday, and I was astonished when the UPS truck made a stop at my door that afternoon with a square, flat box. Inside was a small holly wreath and a birthday card from Lindy. She'd written, "December holly for May. Happy birthday, dear friend."

I stared at the wreath for a long time. Then I found a hammer and stepped outside. I pounded a big nail into the front door and hung the wreath.

I stepped down the front walk to admire it from the street just as Janine came out to work on the icy patches that had been making her front walk treacherous for days.

"Hi, May," she called cheerfully. "Happy New Year."

I waved.

"Is that a new wreath?" she asked. "It's lovely."

"Thank you," I said. "It's from a friend."

She looked surprised, but I just waved again and went inside.

I spent that snowy evening making more travel plans and ordering bulbs. Katharine White, who didn't change her clothes to garden because she thought it inappropriate to "dress down to the plants," loved gardening catalogs, too. She said it was like no other reading experience because you read for pleasure and knowledge, while at the same time planning the future. In that way, while the snow fell, I crossed into the new year.

Nesting

March 10

Dear May,

Just want to say again that I'm sorry things were so
bumpy with Sara. She's only four, but strong-willed
and opinionated, as you know. I imagine she's
missing the feeling of her mom and dad together
and found the presence of another adult, in what
must have seemed to her like her dad's space, very
threatening. He's been sleeping in the guest room
for some time.

But I'm writing to let you know that Sara
loves the bumblebee you brought her! We play a
game to remember where it came from, and

when I name you, she laughs. So in spite of all
the difficulties, you clearly made a good
impression.

I hope we can plan another visit again soon. I'm
glad you reached out; it was great to see you. Next
time I'll show you more of Seattle.

Love, Neera

P.S. I'm enclosing a postcard that came for you
just after you left.

NEERA LIVED IN the suburbs of Seattle and had given me directions for a taxi from the airport. My flight was delayed by
thunderstorms, so while the plans had originally involved my
getting there in time to go with Neera to pick up Sara from
preschool, I ended up arriving after dinner. Neera answered the
door in a wooden mask, which was, she explained, part of the
bath-time routine. I was a little disappointed. In accordance
with epic tradition, someone was getting a bath, but it wasn't
me and I'd been on a plane for five hours. She handed me another mask, which was held in place by biting on a little ledge
at the mouth, rendering conversation difficult. I asked after
Adam and Neera removed her mask to say he was out. Then
Sara streaked down the center hall and Neera went after her,
leaving me in the hallway with my mask.

It was one of the more unusual arrivals I've experienced, and I'm not sure I'd recommend it, but it did break the ice. Neera and I hadn't seen each other since before Sara was born, and within minutes I was helping to carry the child to the tub.

"Hi," I said to her. "I'm May."

"I know," Sara said. Then she whispered something to Neera. When neither of them filled me in, I asked what she said.

Sara shook her head, but Neera told me anyway. "She said you have more starlight in your hair than I do."

So Penelope had Athena boosting her beauty at opportune moments; I had a four-year-old telling me I was grayer than her mother.

I assumed Adam would be returning later, but after Sara was tucked in and we'd eaten dinner and Neera started to open a second bottle of wine, I asked after him again. Neera, Adam, and I met in the first month of college, during those anxious weeks of new friend making that most seemed to enjoy and I survived. When Adam and Neera started dating in our second year, I wasn't surprised. When they got married after graduation and Neera asked me to be her maid of honor, I was. I'd assumed she had closer friends.

Neera put down the bottle and looked at me across the kitchen table. I held my breath and thought, until she spoke, that Adam was sick, or in the hospital, or that something awful had happened. She'd always kept her hair in a short, neat bob, which was now ragged and grown out to her shoulders. This suddenly seemed like a bad sign.

She said, "Adam and I are nesting."

Unfamiliar with this term, yet painfully aware from Neera's expression that this was not good news, I didn't say anything. When it was clear that it would have to be explained to me, Neera resumed her work with the wine bottle.

"We're getting divorced," she said. "Nesting is when you keep things as stable as possible for the children. They stay in the nest, while Adam and I rotate in and out."

Fly seemed the better verb, but I didn't say anything. "What happened?"

"He had an affair. Twice, actually. We got through the first time, started counseling, then he started seeing her again."

"I'm so sorry, Neera."

Neera shook her head and poured us more wine. "I know you're friends with us both, and if you want to see him, you can. I'm not interested in sides. I just want this whole thing to be over."

"No, that's okay. I came to see you."

Neera burst into tears.

When a friend is suffering, it seems you have three options: You can sit silently with her, you can make suggestions, or you can share heartache from your own life. None of the three is as simple as it sounds. I knew someone in college who was so full of advice it was exhausting to share problems with her. You left with a small treatise of self-improvement ideas and the urge to lie down. Share too many of your own stories and tragedy starts to feel competitive. I opted for the first approach and put my hand on her warm back while she sobbed.

Neera had always been the kind of person who warns you of

the mess, then you step into her dorm room or house and it's immaculate. This time, though, it was not. In fact, it felt a little like a nest. But the only difference between human homes and the homes of the rest of the animal kingdom is compartmentalization. It isn't warmth or durability or a penchant for decoration that distinguishes our homemaking; it is merely that we organize our space into different areas.

House or nest, I was going to have to get another hostess gift. I'd brought a set of blue nesting bowls, which seemed now a distinctly bad choice.

Before we went up to bed, I asked if she'd like help cleaning the kitchen. Neera looked around, as if surprised to see it wasn't clean. "Why?" she said.

"I don't know," I said. "Some people like the closure."

"I don't need closure on the day. There's just going to be another one in the morning."

SARA WOKE ME UP by very quietly and very deliberately pulling each of the blankets off my bed. I tried to make a game of it, but Sara was serious. She did not want me in the bed, in the room, in the house. I ended up standing in a corner of the kitchen while Neera made coffee and tried to reason with her. Nothing worked until Neera proposed a walk to the playground. I was genuinely surprised. Sara seemed so adult in her demands. What on earth would she do at a playground?

But she liked to swing. And she specifically liked me to push her on the swing, so that's what I did, trying all the while to shake the feeling that Sara, as she couldn't get rid of me, was pleased to be putting me to use.

It was a windy, relatively mild day and everything was wet from the day before. Neera kept a towel in her bag to dry the slides and swings, which I thought was very clever of her. We ran into a couple Neera and Adam knew, but while the woman came over to say hello, her partner stayed on his phone. He looked up once with an irritating half-smile.

Neera introduced me as an old friend from college and the woman said, "Oh, so you must be one of Sara's godmothers!"

I looked at Neera, who just smiled.

"We love Sara," the woman said. "She's such a riot." We all turned to see Sara getting ready to do a somersault down the slide.

Neera said, "Excuse me," and rushed to stop her.

"Nice to meet you. Have a lovely visit," the woman said, steering her daughter to another part of the playground.

"She's English," Neera said, returning from the slide. "The godparent thing is a big deal to her."

"Does Sara have godparents?" I asked.

She hesitated. "Yes. Friends from here."

I was not hurt, just surprised.

"I really didn't think you'd be interested," Neera said, and that did seem fair, though for some reason it made me a little sad.

"Is there somewhere we can get ice cream on the way home?" I asked.

We ate our cones while we walked, and in front of Neera's

house I noticed her garden needed attention. It looked as if the fall cleanup had been aborted. Perennials that should have been cut back before winter were wilted on the ground, several shrubs needed pruning before they started to bud. An eclectic array of ceramic pots lined the front steps, too many for my taste, all of them holding soggy, dead plants.

"Do you have a landscaper?" I asked.

"No, we . . . I do it myself," Neera said.

"That's great! I'd love to help. I could do some weeding for you tomorrow."

Neera stared at me. "You do not need to do that."

"But I'd enjoy it. I like weeding."

"May, I don't want you to weed for me."

"We could do it together, with Sara."

Neera surveyed the front of her house. She walked to the steps and straightened a few pots, pulled dead plants out of a couple more and dropped them in the grass. "No, I don't care and I don't have the time."

Just as it is unwise to offer unsolicited parenting advice, so, too, gardening tips. I conceded, but the next morning I couldn't help myself. I woke up early because of the jet lag, and lying in bed thinking about that neglected garden was torture. I got dressed quickly and went out to do a little work before Neera was awake. I don't think she even noticed.

FOR SOME PEOPLE, the presence of a visitor acts as a kind of stimulant, inspiring outings and fine meals. Lindy is like this.

For others, a visitor registers as grit in the gears, leaving everyone a bit sluggish and on edge.

Neera fell into this category. When the next day dawned overcast and rainy again, I encouraged her to catch up on a few errands while I watched Sara, who'd warmed to me just enough to make this possible. We put on Sara's favorite show, *Angelina Ballerina*, and after several episodes, I began to feel the lulling comfort of children's programming: one problem at a time; you see it coming from a mile away; you watch it rise, evolve, and resolve all in less time than it takes to bake a batch of cookies. And friendship, though it may be challenged during the half hour, is always golden and secure by the end.

Between episodes Sara accused me of liking the color gray. Her evidence: my gray jeans, my pearl-gray scarf, and my steel-gray coat in the hall. I suspect she thought I'd deny the charge, but I didn't, and she seemed to find this interesting. "My favorite color is pink," she said.

"You may feel differently when you're older," I said.

"No, I won't," she said. "I'm not boring."

Then the dancing mouse show started again.

I needed a break, so I left the family room and wandered through the kitchen and into the formal front room of the house. I don't understand this kind of room. Houses have had best rooms or front parlors for centuries, but in modern times they seem to have become especially useless. Once reserved for special occasions or holidays or a death in the family, no one ever particularly wants to gather there now. In Lindy's house, she'd told me, the dog had often pooped in the front room when he was a puppy. When I asked Neera about hers, she waved her hand dismissively. "I don't have time to spend in there," she said.

I sat down on Neera's best couch. It was surprisingly comfortable. There were real curtains in here, ones you might call drapes, and two matching lamps and some expensive-looking candlesticks on a small mantel over a gas fireplace. It was very quiet. I couldn't hear the television and the traffic outside was muffled. I couldn't even hear a dog barking. I checked my phone to see if Neera had texted to say when she'd be back, and it felt like the loneliest activity in the world, sitting alone in a formal front room, checking your phone.

When the doorbell rang, Sara came barreling down the hall to answer it. I was right behind her, but she opened the door.

"Daddy!"

Adam didn't look as miserable as I thought he might. He had a scruffy beard, which suited him, and the same kind eyes I remembered. The only sign of stress might have been that he'd gained some weight.

"May," he said, as if we'd seen each other last week. "I didn't know you were here."

"I didn't know you were nesting."

"Neera didn't tell you?"

"Not before I got here, no."

"What's nesting?" Sara asked.

I froze. Adam winced and rubbed his forehead. "Making a cozy home for you, sweet pea," he said. "I love you."

"Watch Angelina with me!" She began pulling him toward the back of the house and I stepped out of the way. I knew first-hand how strong she was.

Adam stumbled a few steps forward, then stopped. "I can't, sweet pea. I just came by to pick up something I forgot. I can't stay."

"Why can't you stay?" Sara asked.

"Neera's out," I offered.

"That's not how this works," Adam snapped, then looked so sad I tried to help.

"Because I'm taking you to the park!" I said to Sara.

She looked at me skeptically. "That's not what Mommy said."

Adam knelt down to her height. "I'm going to see you in a few days and we're going to do lots of fun things, okay? But right now I have to go."

"Okay," she said, and took my hand. "You watch with me." And so I did.

Adam found the jacket he'd left upstairs and blew a kiss to Sara before he left. He waved to me and I waved back, which felt a little like a betrayal of Neera, but I didn't know what else to do.

I had a late-afternoon cup of coffee in the hope of staying awake through Sara's bath and bedtime so Neera and I could talk, but Neera was so tired by the end of the day it felt kinder to let her go to bed than to keep her up with questions. I'm certain Penelope would have done the same, sensing another woman's home in crisis.

The last day of my visit we didn't have a plan. The rain had stopped, but Sara didn't want to go to the playground again. Neera and I were lingering over coffee when suddenly Neera jumped up and said, "I know!"

Before I could object, she'd booked three tickets for us to see the flower show in town. Under the circumstances, it seemed like a heroic act of friendship, so I refrained from telling her that a flower show in a convention center is like a ship in a bottle, strange and unnatural. The smells from food vendors often overpower the flowers, and the crowds can be shocking. A flower show is to gardening what the runway is to fashion: beyond the reach of mortals. People go to gawk.

I wasn't optimistic, but touring a flower show with an eager four-year-old in a ballet skirt turned out to have some advantages. The lines around the gardens were long, but someone would notice Sara trying to see on tiptoe and wave us in. Was it the well-dressed ladies in hats and feathers who smiled at us and let Sara cut the line? Not at all. It was the men in jeans, the landscapers, the real-life installers, I guessed, of gardens like the ones we were looking at, who moved aside and said, "Go ahead. Absolutely. Let her see." A few older women told Sara she looked as pretty as a flower in her pink dress. Sara mostly remained mute, which I admired.

Twice Neera and I were reminiscing about college when she thought she spotted the woman Adam was seeing in the crowd. Her face went white and she grabbed my arm. Both times she was wrong. "Same posture," she said once, shaking her head. And, "She has that coat." Both times we lost the thread of our conversation and couldn't recover it.

After lunch, which was dominated by what Sara would and wouldn't eat, we saw a few more gardens, then headed briefly to the window-box competition, where I would have lingered, but one look at Neera's face told me we were done. I made an exception to my cut-flower rule and bought Neera and Sara each a posy of pink and yellow *Ranunculus asiaticus* before we left. Sara accepted hers with gratifying solemnity, quite taken with the tight folds of concentric petals. On the drive home, she fell asleep holding her flowers.

"Thank you," I said to Neera. "That was a lovely afternoon. You didn't have to do that for me."

"I wanted to. And, really, it was something for Sara and me to do, too. I worry about not doing enough fun things with her. Somehow Adam is the fun parent."

I knew that as soon as we got back to the house we'd begin the evening routine, so I whispered, "Neera, how are you doing?"

She shook her head. "I don't know. I can't answer that. But today is a good day."

"What happens after nesting?" I asked. "Do you know what you're waiting for?"

She glanced at Sara in the rearview mirror. "Things to get easier."

"I understand that," I said. "Me, too." I thought she might ask me to explain, but she didn't.

"Did you know people will underestimate the weight of a

heavy backpack before climbing a steep hill if they're standing next to a friend?"

"Aww," Neera said. "That's nice."

I looked out my window. Every stripped tire looked like roadkill.

After a minute Neera said, "Actually, that really is something."

"I thought so," I said.

That night I packed up my things and so did Neera. She would be staying with local friends until her next turn nesting. In the morning, I left the guest room exactly as I'd found it. We dropped Sara at her preschool on the way to the airport; Adam would pick her up in the afternoon and for the next week and a half, Sara and the house were his.

When Neera hugged me good-bye, she said, "I'm here if you need me."

"Me, too," I said.

I knew we both meant it, but on the other hand, we would make each other ask.

March 14

Dear Neera,

Our notes must have crossed in the mail. I hope by now you've received mine and know what a lovely time I had. Please don't worry: I proposed the visit

on short notice and you were brave to take me up
on it. You shared your home, which is never easy,
no matter the circumstances, and were a gracious
host. Thank you for a wonderful, memorable
weekend. I only wish I could have helped you more.

Yours, May

P. S. Tell Sara I'm reconsidering pink. She'll
understand.

ALLEGEDLY WARMTH, cheeriness, friendliness, and strength
are distinct from one another and your likability is largely determined by how much of each you project. The definition of
warmth is how easily you convey you have something in common with another person. Rereading my note, I worried I was
better at being warm in writing than in person.

The Steiff bumblebee I brought Sara had been mine as a
child. Most of my Steiff collection is boxed up in the basement,
but I keep a few of the bees nestled into the African violets on
the windowsill behind my kitchen sink. They're black and yellow, about two inches long, with two pieces of felt for wings
and black yarn antennae. I have two left, and they sit there with
the pink tape measure and now also a little stone bird paper-
weight. It did not occur to me until I was flying home that a
stone bird from a place where a broken family is trying hard to

make a nest is a little grim. But what's grimmer than the bumblebee? Her stinger is barbed so it will stick under the skin after it has pierced you. When she attempts to fly off, her intestines are pulled out and she'll die, unless you can find a way to dislodge the stinger gently.

Postcards

The postcard Neera had included was from Leo. My father told me he'd given him the address. The picture was a view of the university grounds showing my yew, though that wouldn't mean anything to Leo, and the text in its entirety read "Signed up for an extension class at the university. Plant Identification. Starting in two weeks. Leo."

I put it on the windowsill behind my sink.

I'd already been to El Puerto with my father since returning from Neera's, but hadn't mentioned the postcard because I hadn't gotten it yet. I'd complimented him on the whiskey barrel planters he'd placed at the corners of the promenade. They were real wood ones, not the fake plastic kind, and I thought they were a good choice. I warned him not to fill them completely with soil, but to use empty plastic bottles in a layer along the bottom to improve drainage. He thanked me, and my father and I ate our dinner.

After Neera's, I had some busy weeks at work. Blake had been asked to help create a university farm. He'd anticipated this—our administration was slower than most at recognizing the changing social landscape—and we'd been discussing plans for more than a year. Now we knew where it would be— one of the founder's historic homes was ceding acreage from its extensive flower gardens. There was already a placard that read "Future site of the University Farm, which will enhance students' overall educational experience as well as their understanding of the sustainability challenges that will affect their adult lives."

Blake told me the university wanted an organic garden, a flock of laying hens, a number of beehives, and a small herd of goats.

"A tunnel greenhouse is also a possibility," he said.

"Is there enough room for all that?" I asked.

"No," Blake said. He rarely wasted words.

I WENT BACK OFTEN to the café where I'd seen the elderly friends who met there for coffee every day. I'd learned their names were Maris and Helen, and I liked to sit near them. They didn't talk a lot, and when they did it was mostly about people they both knew, often illnesses related to those people. Maris, the small and thin one, liked to smoke a cigarette, for which they would both move outside and sit next to a pot of purple pansies. If it was cold, and we were having a chilly March, it took them awhile to get their coats on. Sometimes

Maris read the daily horoscope out loud, her voice as low and gravelly as you'd imagine for a lifelong smoker. Helen, the tall and heavy one, listened to the brief horoscopes and together they discussed each one as if it were an important piece of news. Their mutual friends nearly covered the zodiac. If they hit a horoscope for which they couldn't remember someone, they called out to the barista, "When were you born?" All the baristas knew them, the café owner knew them, other shopkeepers on the street knew them. They argued sometimes, but it never amounted to anything.

When little, friends play house in order to pretend to be family, which is ironic because the beauty of friends is that they are chosen, not given. Should siblings play friends? And do we *make* friends or *find* them? Emily Dickinson thought the best verb was *enact*.

One morning in late March, inspired by Leo, I decided to send my brother a postcard. He emailed once in a while with my father, but he and I hadn't really been in touch for years. A postcard would travel publicly by U.S. postal service across three thousand miles, but the act of buying, writing, stamping, and sending it suddenly felt more intimate than anything else I could do. This was a broadcast to one, after all, not one and a crowd of follower-friends.

The Anneville diversity festival was in full swing. Anneville is very proud of this annual festival and the daffodils and tulips were in full bloom, so people were out in droves. I made my way through the crowds to the university gift shop, where I chose a postcard showing a photograph of the town square in winter. I found it in the seasonal discount pile: one red cardinal perched on a snow-laden evergreen branch, looking like a forgotten Christmas bauble. On the other side I wrote only, "Do they have Christmas in France?" which was a line from a movie that had made us laugh when we were kids.

That night I dreamed my brother and I were playing house. For some reason it involved a lot of cleaning. I was walking around barefoot and he was surprised. He looked down at my feet and said he couldn't do that anymore because it hurt too much. I told him it hurt me, too, but that I'd practiced. I wiggled my toes.

Then suddenly, in that nonlinear way of dreams, we were walking in a pine forest. A guide appeared and took us to a dollhouse in the woods. He pointed out holes left by Revolutionary War—era musket fire, or so he said. My brother studied the bullet holes, while I marveled at all the beds. There was at least one in each room, all different colors. And that was the end of the dream.

— House Bound —

To me *shelter* is a word that leans more toward survival than luxury, and yet it's the term for magazines with an editorial focus on interior design, architecture, home furnishings, and gardening. In other words, nice things not essential for survival. The term was first used this way in 1946 in reference to a magazine called *Your Own Home*, which was devoted to the very real problem of postwar low-cost housing. "Shelter magazine" grew into a misnomer over time.

Shelter magazines assume boundless energy, and often boundless wealth, but not always. Energy, though, is nonnegotiable. You have to want to work on your house. You have to ignore the fact that a house during most of mankind's time on earth was a necessity, not a display case of prized personal possessions and decorating prowess. The spaces were crowded and multiuse. Beds were shared.

A house becomes a *home* when a person or a group of people

has an emotional attachment to it. A house is a physical thing that is built with wood and bricks, furnished with furniture and carpets, while a *home* takes time and is built with memories. Shelter magazines, however, would like to convince you that the right colors and fabrics can help.

If instead the shelter magazines covered subjects such as tracing new worry paths across your floorboards, redecorating for the invalid, or area rugs to cover blood stains, I might be more interested. Housekeeping for the grief addled? Gardening for the undone? Then I'd consider a subscription.

But perhaps I'm bitter. My parents never had enough money to redecorate. I learned that you conform your life to the space you have, just like the earliest cave dwellers: This one will do! But now most people tear out perfectly serviceable kitchens and bathrooms simply to re-create them in a style they prefer. Now people are bent on designing a space to suit their lives.

Here's a word: *reside,* from the Latin *sidere,* "to sink or settle." Can you change where you reside because someone died? It's such a modern idea to even contemplate it. Until the eighteenth century, the idea of having comfort in the home was so unfamiliar, no word existed for the condition. *Comfortable* meant merely "capable of being consoled." Prior to World War I, the drawing room was often referred to as the "death room" because it was where the bodies of loved ones were laid out. After the world wars, the shelter magazine known as *Ladies' Home Journal* suggested it was high time for a "living room" and the term took hold.

As did my father and I, though he moved to the basement

and I still walk through the rest of the house now and then burning sage.

MY MOTHER WAS DIFFERENT around other people. She never, that I can remember, had lunch with a friend. She never met someone in the evening for a drink or a movie. Even before she went upstairs, my mother liked rainy days because they seemed to reduce expectations; the rest of the world slowed to her pace. I was always at pains to express joy in sunlight, hoping this was the way forward, worried about the trajectory she was on.

And yet she is the one who gave me, Lindy, and Vanessa a framed picture of us together at our high school graduation. She made copies, bought frames, wrapped the boxes, and brought them to a graduation party Vanessa's parents hosted. No one else gave us a present that celebrated our friendship like that. Why did I never ask her, But where are your friends?

Who are the recluses and what are their reasons? Who are the people who decide to limit their frame of reference? The walls of her room became a boundary, the door frame a threshold it became difficult for me to cross. I stood there often, watching her sleep. Marlene Dietrich was bedridden for the last eleven years of her life, Proust the last three. People feel sorry for the house bound, but it can be a position of strength, a refusal to meet the world on its terms. Emily Dickinson was a recluse; she gardened at night. Emily Brontë, Greta Garbo. The recluse decides when and to whom she will speak, access is limited.

At times I felt that the children of immigrants were lucky, not in so many matters of social and economic security, obviously, but in the matter of understanding their parents. Behind those parents stood a whole country, somewhere to go for deeper insight into who they were before they came to America. Who was my mother before she went upstairs? I barely know and there is no place to go where I can ask questions. I have a few stories. I have a memory of her wearing a yellow shirt in sunlight when I was young and her hair was very long. I have the year we took walks and the autumn she taught me to drive.

I'm not unhappy, I only want to understand what happened because I, too, have spent a day upstairs, drifting in and out of sleep, staring at the light shifting across the room, holding a book but not reading, and still felt by dinnertime ready for more sleep. Who's to say there won't be more such days? I have a fear of rooms where people spend too much time, especially if there is a bed in them. Xavier de Maistre's book-length memoir, *Voyage Around My Room,* is witty to some, but reads like a horror story to me. When you are alone in a room, time is slow and not particularly nice. It will wait in the dusty corner and taunt and try to convince you there's not much point in doing anything. Stay, rest. Wait it out. Penelope waited upstairs. So did my mother. I do not want to do the same.

Fortnight Friends

In April Sue and I worked in the beds around the library, filled mostly with mature rhododendron and hydrangea, some of my favorite plants on campus. The tall winter stems were hanging with curled, wilted leaves that looked like sleeping bats. We were cutting them back and mulching.

"Have you seen the paper?" Sue asked.

"Not today. Why?"

"That reporter is either trying to make you famous, or . . ." Sue frequently got herself into these comparative binds.

"What?"

"She's written a piece about some rich guy in Paris who was inspired by your hashtag." Here Sue stopped shoveling mulch and stretched her back.

"Not mine."

"Yeah, well, he sold his apartment and most of his belongings, everything except what he could fit into a suitcase—an extremely expensive suitcase—and a leather backpack. He just turned forty and has decided to downsize his life and focus more on his friendships and experiences. Sound familiar?"

"How much was the suitcase?"

"Fifteen hundred dollars! He's a tech entrepreneur or something. He doesn't have a home or a base of any kind. He just travels from friend to friend."

"Oh. Does he have a lot?"

"The article didn't say."

We worked for a few minutes.

"Aren't you curious how it's going?" Sue asked.

"I guess."

"His friends are miserable! Apparently he keeps terrible hours and the wife of the first friend ended up making his bed and doing his laundry. That visit lasted a week. The next one, where he ended up just *taking* his friend's clothes, only lasted three days. It's just so typical. He took your idea—which, Maria says, and, I don't know, maybe she's wrong, but she says it's about visiting your friends to see their lives, not to impose your life on theirs—and turned it into something else, something that's all about him."

I was moved by the idea of Maria and Sue discussing me. "Well, it's a work in progress," I said.

I almost told her I'd named Grendel, but I was stuck on the cost of the other suitcase. I was also impressed by Maria's understanding. I didn't remember outlining my thinking so clearly. But it had occurred to me that one of the questions I most wanted to ask my friends was: Can I see an average day in your life right now? A real day, not one curated for social media or filled with the best activities to entertain a visitor. On the one hand, it's a simple question. On the other, it's almost too intimate. And it might be impossible, because the presence of a visitor changes a day, no matter how close the friends are. Destinations are planned, observations made. It's the way we function when people come to see us, often because the trust required to really let someone see your life is rare. Even Henry James felt the need to take good friends for a view of the sea when they came to spend a day with him.

"Well, I hope he has a lot of friends," I said.

"He won't when this little experiment is over."

Sue lost her footing and stumbled against a rhododendron, bending to the breaking point a long stalk with many buds. "Shit," she said softly to the plant. "I'm sorry."

I READ THE ARTICLE later and everything Sue had said was accurate. I did a little Googling and realized that the hashtag had persisted into the new year. It had survived the backlash and was now a fairly regular meme, due in large part to the efforts of Abby Mara, who was now a stringer for a major newspaper.

Mara had gotten people talking again about the Dunbar number—the maximum number of people with whom any individual can maintain stable relationships—and how, despite predictions, it hadn't gotten any bigger in the age of social media. Related articles discussed how social isolation seemed to be killing us and how the platitudes of contemporary friendship (the status update, the tweet, the hashtag) were not enough because it is ultimately shared, face-to-face experience that we need to feel understood. Someone had shown that a touch on the arm between friends increased endorphin production by three times the rate of a heart-eyes emoji. The term "radical friendship" had been coined and was being bandied about in essays short and long. And for the first time in its history, Facebook was having a sustained dip in its share price. With personal days, vacation days, or by whatever means they had, people were making plans to spend more time with friends.

If radical friendship and the popularity of #fortnightfriend continued to grow, it seemed possible someone would eventually want to come and stay with me. Before bed, I took a good look at the guest room and concluded it needed work. For one thing, Hester had been sleeping in there and the bedspread was covered with cat fur. She was curled up now against the pillows and raised her head to look at me while I stood in the doorway. Outside I could hear a spring robin, a melancholy sound more searching than song to me. It's not my favorite harbinger of the season.

"Come on," I said to Hester, and carried her upstairs to sleep in my room.

Banyan Tree (*Ficus benghalensis*)

As the yew is to the churchyard, the banyan is to the marketplace: For centuries people have gathered in its deep, wide shade to barter and trade. It would be a good memorial, but we'd have no luck with it in Anneville. They are easily damaged by frost and are therefore best grown in warmer climates. Another problem is that the banyan requires a lot of space. It should not be planted near foundations, driveways, streets, or homes, as its canopy and aerial root system can spread quite far. The largest banyan tree in the United States is in Lahaina, Hawaii. It was planted in 1837 as an eight-foot sapling and is now sixty feet tall with sixteen major trunks and a canopy circumference of a quarter mile. One thousand people can stand in its shade.

It is possible to grow a banyan as a houseplant. They are surprisingly well adapted to indoor environments and are often used in bonsai, as the shoot tips can be pinched back to promote branching and control size.

But I'm not going to mention this to my father. As a memorial, this would be enormously problematic. If I became sick or incapacitated, bequeathing it would be difficult. Better to let nature do the maintenance.

The Airport Road

The first Thursday in May my father and I missed our dinner at El Puerto because he wasn't feeling well, so I suggested Sunday brunch at a new place, his choice. He picked Cracker Barrel.

"When did we get one of those?" I asked, unable to conceal my disdain.

"It's good," my father said. "I've been a couple of times."

"When?"

"With Janine's family. She invited me."

We took the airport road. The pear trees (*Pyrus calleryana*) in the median, to which I have a mild allergy, were in bloom. When I was little, I called them popcorn trees because of all the small white flowers. Now every year my father points at them, I nod, and we both smile. I wondered if he'd told Janine that story when she drove him on the airport road. In conflicts around the world, it's very important who controls the road to the airport. Sometimes the road is shut down and that's always a sign the conflict is escalating.

At the restaurant the wait was ninety minutes. My father said he wasn't hungry anyway, so we drove home. I made us eggs and toast and we took sections of the newspaper out to the backyard to enjoy the mild weather.

Before I took my first bite, I heard a thud. I lowered the paper and saw a starling on the grass about ten feet away. It moved its head once and then was still.

My father looked up from his paper. "The little guy snapped his neck on that cable wire."

We stared at the bird. A warm breeze ruffled a wing feather.

"Does this kind of thing happen often?" I asked.

"Well, Janine and I buried another one behind the mock orange last week."

My father turned back to his breakfast, but I'd lost my appetite. When he was finished, we buried the bird behind the mock orange (*Philadelphus coronaris*), right next to the other fresh little mound.

A FEW DAYS LATER Janine and I pulled out of our driveways at the same time. Janine drives a Honda minivan. She has two children under five, one dog, two cats, and a husband whose shifts at the hospital are incompatible with all of that. And yet she has time to spend with my father. Leo told me he remembers American tourists coming to his town when he was a boy. They worried excessively about the roaming, homeless cats.

They wanted to feed them, name them. What a luxury, his mother would say, to have time to worry about cats.

At the stop sign at the end of the street, Janine turned right over the railroad bridge and I followed. As we approached the light at Founders Avenue, she turned right again. She was headed toward the university. I guessed she was going to Barracks Mall, a frequent destination of young mothers as it has both a twenty-four-hour pharmacy and one of the most popular cafés in town. I held the wheel at ten and two and looked straight ahead. Janine was wearing sunglasses and I couldn't tell from the angle of her head if she was glancing in her rearview mirror or not. I turned a couple of times to admire the dogwoods (*Cornus florida*) in the median. They were just starting to bloom, and while I never would have planted them in a pink-and-white alternating pattern, they were lovely.

We drove the length of Founders Avenue. She was going ten miles over the speed limit, but I kept pace. At the end of the road I prepared to keep straight, anticipating her upcoming left to Barracks, but she took the right fork toward the hospital and merged fast.

I was surprised. The children weren't in the car with her. Had something happened to one of them? Or her husband? It also seemed at least possible she was pregnant again. Maybe something was wrong?

She pulled into the visitor's lot and I took the spot next to her. She was not in a rush to get out of the car. In fact, she was finishing her breakfast. She stopped chewing and did a cinematic double take when she saw me. We held each other's gaze while simultaneously lowering the car windows between us. I watched as the reflection of the sky in her driver's side window disappeared, revealing Janine's young and shiny face. She had very good skin. She must have seen a reflection of the hospital building in my passenger-side window give way to my face, which had a spring sunburn.

"Is everything okay?" I asked.

At first Janine looked surprised and almost happy to see me, then confused. She finished chewing and swallowed. "Why? What happened?"

"You're at the hospital."

"I volunteer here."

"Oh, that's great."

"I read to the kids in the Ambulatory Care unit. Sometimes I do a shift in the gift shop."

"That's so great," I said. "That's . . . really helpful."

"What are you doing here?"

"Oh, I just wanted to thank you for helping my father bury the bird."

"That was so sad," she said.

"And taking him to lunch?" I'd meant to suppress the question mark, but it forced its way out.

Janine frowned a little. "We really enjoy spending time with him."

"That's great," I said, painfully aware of how many times I'd used that word.

"He's great," she said. "He gave me some of your mock orange branches and told me how to force them."

I nodded.

She glanced at the clock in her car. "I should go. So, um, May, you followed me to thank me?"

"Oh, no," I said. "I'm visiting a friend. A friend who's in the hospital." I looked past her car to the rows of hospital windows.

"I hope everything's okay."

"Me, too," I said, and started preparing to get out of the car. "Anyway, thanks for spending time with my father."

I could see in my peripheral vision that she was staring at me. "You know, sometimes they just need to feel useful."

"They?"

She sighed. "You know what I mean."

"My father's name is Earl."

THAT NIGHT I ASKED MY FATHER if he'd like to try Cracker Barrel again the following Sunday. We could leave earlier and beat the rush. Confusing it with Crate & Barrel, however, I called it Cracker & Barrel. My father either didn't notice or didn't mind. He accepted happily.

Mock Orange

The first time I smelled the blossom of the orange tree (*Citrus sinensis*) I was thirteen years old. It's one of the most fragrant flowers in the world, and in Florida millions of the waxy, white flowers perfume the air in the spring. My mother, brother, and I stepped out of the Fort Lauderdale airport into that sweet-smelling air. We'd come for the christening of my new cousin, my mother's sister's new baby. The christening had become the occasion for a rare family reunion at my maternal grandmother's house.

I knew some things about my grandmother. I knew that on my mother's eighteenth birthday a friend of the family gave her a beautiful watch that my grandmother liked so much she took it for herself. I knew that when I was six she wanted me to say "I've had an elegant sufficiency" before I could be excused from the table. I knew that when I was in elementary school I often came home to find my mother crying in the kitchen, a letter in her lap, the return address always her mother's.

The first two days of the trip passed comfortably. Everyone ate breakfast at different times and occupied themselves for the morning. The walls of the condo were covered with photographs of my grandmother in her prime. In most of them she looked like a 1940s movie star, which she had been, briefly. There were only a few pictures that included my mother, but I understood that was because my mother hadn't come to live with her until she was eight years old. Before that, my mother lived with her father, my grandmother's first husband, and didn't know her mother at all.

The night before the christening, I came to the dinner table with my hair down. At the time, I had long hair and usually wore it in a ponytail. I'd been swimming that afternoon, though, and when I got back to the condo I'd showered and washed my hair in order to be ready for the christening the next day. I brushed it out neatly and left it down to dry.

When my grandmother saw me, she told me to leave and come back with my hair up. I hesitated, unsure whether she was serious, but then she shouted it was rude to wear one's hair down at dinner, she couldn't believe I didn't know better, I had no manners. I looked at my mother, but she nodded at me to go.

I returned to the table with the highest ponytail I could manage, so tight it was hurting my scalp. I concentrated on the candle flames and listened to my grandmother's voice. She spoke in bursts that waned as they lost momentum, as if the initial idea were long harbored but began to fade as soon as it was released. She attacked everyone at the table. It wasn't until the end of dinner, when my aunt started clearing and my grandmother demanded another bottle of wine, that I began to understand.

My memories of the last two days are hazy. I remember the blue dress my grandmother wore the day of the christening; it matched her beautiful eyes. I remember the new lavender dress my mother had bought me as a surprise. My grandmother drank all afternoon and by dinnertime served us a burned casserole, helping herself to bites from the ladle between slapping portions onto our plates. No one bothered to light the candles.

The next day it thundered all morning. My grandfather drove us to the airport, his mood quiet but not gloomy. The last thing he said to my mother was "Your mother loves you." She had been about to open the car door and step out, but when he said this she paused. She looked pale and sad, the way I grew accustomed to seeing her. I thought she was going to respond, and I waited. Years later it occurred to me that when someone says what my grandfather did, what they mean, what would be far more accurate, is "She is trying to love you as best she can." This might be okay with you, or it might not. It might not be what you need at all.

After a moment, my mother nodded and stepped out of the car into the rain.

A few years later my grandmother died, and sometime after that so did my mother, and now I am forty years old, older than my mother was then. I don't have a daughter and I don't know if I ever will. But if I do, we will not carry this sadness forward. I'm tired of holding it.

I DON'T LOVE the bank of mock orange behind the house on Todd Lane. Mock orange is not a tree, it's a shrub, but its flowers have a similar sweet scent. Gardening catalogs will tell you it's an old favorite, perhaps not fitting for a more modern landscape, but sure to bring up much nostalgia in a more traditional setting. You can decide if you want that or not.

Arbotchery

Most people can't identify more than three trees local to their area. Maybe every profession has something equivalent that leaves its practitioners stunned. Builders might marvel at my inability to distinguish between wrenches, for example. But trees are some of the most extraordinary living things on earth. So are blue whales, but few people get to see them. Unless you live in a desert, you probably see a tree every day. It's only because trees are common that we don't appreciate them, and yet if they weren't common, our planet would be uninhabitable, at least by humans as we recognize them. Some trees can absorb 40 percent of the water they need from fog and have bark thick enough to withstand the heat of a forest fire. Yet Samuel Johnson defined a tree as "a large vegetable rising, with one woody stem, to a considerable height," a dreadful description from an otherwise great writer. It seems the trees' plight is to be always underappreciated by humans while working the hardest of any plant on earth for them. We cut them down, we poison them, we introduce disease and destructive pests. But we also plant them when someone is born, we plant them when someone dies. We want them to measure and commemorate our lives, even as the way we live hurts them.

An example: it is possible to do the needed pruning around power lines without making bad cuts to the trees, but the people who do the work are often paid by the mile and move too fast. The resulting tree shapes can be troubling, not to mention harmful. A few years ago Blake and I started documenting the worst local examples of what we named *arbotchery*, the severe and heartless pruning of trees around wires, leaving them stunted and misshapen forever.

The new owners of the Goulds' house had recently taken out a badly arbotched tree, a decision I had mixed feelings about. On the one hand, the tree looked ridiculous, a small sugar maple (*Acer saccharum*) sheared into a slope. On the other hand, it was a sugar maple. The leaves on the branches that were left turned scarlet every fall.

I asked Blake what he thought. We were filling all the beds around the Green with impatiens (*Impatiens walleriana*).

He shrugged. "Was it unstable?"

"I don't know."

"Hard to say."

Graduation was a week away and the coral and white impatiens were part of the decorations, as fragile as crepe paper. The Super Elfin cultivar was bred in Costa Rica, developed from its native wild form into one of the most popular annuals in the world. I'm not a fan of annuals under the best of circumstances—they are an enormous amount of work for a few weeks of color—and my scorn for the impatiens is second only to my contempt for the petunia, an annual that is equally fragile but also sticky.

"I've been meaning to tell you," Blake said, his voice serious and quiet. "It isn't just the yew. Have you noticed the Douglas fir by the science building? Or the blue spruce by the auditorium?"

I shook my head.

He said recent measurements indicated those trees, too, were growing much faster than they should have been. Blake had talked with several people at the U.S. Forest Service about what he was noticing on campus and they told him recent measurements from around the world showed mature evergreens of all species now regularly exceeding previously recorded height records by twenty to thirty feet.

"Why?" I asked.

Blake settled a little coral impatiens bursting with buds into the soil. "Global warming," he said. "I think they're trying to save us."

I pretended to have some trouble getting the next seedling out of its flat so he wouldn't see my eyes filling with water.

We worked for a while in silence and then, without pausing in his planting, Blake said, "I don't think I'd ever take out a sugar maple."

Postcards

I ran into Philip Gould in front of his old house later that week. I was taking an evening walk, working on my redeemable element game, when I saw him standing in the road with a shovel. I thought he might be missing the sugar maple, but when I got closer I realized he was scraping at a dead rabbit in the road. When he saw me he stopped working and said, in lieu of a greeting, that he'd seen the rabbit hit by a car earlier in the day and had to do something about it.

"Is everything all right?" I asked.

"We had a rabbit in the yard for years. We put food out sometimes. I think this might be the one."

"I'm so sorry," I said.

"Beth is in the hospital."

"Oh, no."

"She had a stroke. A minor one. They think she's going to

be all right." He shook his head. "There's no way of knowing for sure," he said. "About the rabbit, I mean."

I almost said that I'd seen lots of rabbits around Duck Woods, but it wouldn't have been true. The rabbit in the road was so smushed I had to look away. I told him I would be thinking about him and Beth. Philip nodded and went back to his work, lifting as much of the rabbit as he could into a shoebox.

I walked the entire perimeter of Duck Woods—the length of Founders Avenue, left on Huron, which follows the river, left again on Jefferson, which skirts the railroad tracks back up to Todd Lane—but when I got home I could still see that bloody rabbit in my mind.

There were two postcards in the mail. The first one was from my brother. On the back of a photograph of the Pioneer Cabin Tree in Calaveras Big Trees State Park, he'd written, "I loved your postcard." The photo was an old one, black and white, from the time when cars were allowed to drive through the tunnel carved into the tree. The postcard showed a Ford Model T in the tunnel, which was clever. My brother had always been jealous that our mother taught me to drive. "You got her best years," he used to say. And it was true.

I was suddenly so tired I closed the door and sat down right there in the front hall. That part of the house always makes me feel detached, unmoored. Someone else might have tried to meditate, but I can't. Hester came over and sniffed my knee, then circled behind me, bumping the side of her body against my back. She circled and purred until I stood up. Hester wasn't alive when my mother died, but I swear she doesn't like the front hall either. I got her as a kitten a few years afterward and named her for Hestia, goddess of family and home. Hestia was the daughter of Rhea, who, it's interesting to note, had no particular activity under her control.

The front hall isn't large, it's more of a vestibule. If you stand at the front door and look into the house, there is a table and mirror to the right, a center hallway in front of you leading to the living room and kitchen at the back of the house, and to the left is the dining room. The staircase begins in the hall and rises to the left to a landing edged with a balustrade, then turns right up to the second-floor hallway. Off that hallway are three bedrooms and a bathroom. The bedroom I've used since my mother died overlooks the front yard. It was my brother's, and other than taking down his posters so that the walls are bare, I've never decorated it. When Balzac was a poor writer in Paris he lived in a garret and inscribed on his bare walls notes on the things he wanted to own one day. "Rosewood paneling." "Picture by Raphael." I haven't even done that.

I wondered if my brother knew the Pioneer Cabin Tree had fallen a few years ago, felled by a storm. It shattered on impact, but scientists estimated it was more than a thousand years old. I put the postcard on top of my father's tree sheets and decided to see the whole episode as progress.

The second postcard was from Leo.

The Right Evergreen

I'd been avoiding Leo, not sure what to do about his first postcard. My father had kept up his El Puerto schedule, though, and had told me that the restaurant was being threatened by a developer who had not only purchased the whole mall but the dell behind it. He wanted to bulldoze the mall, level the dell, and build a large unit of luxury condominiums. My father said students, fueled by spring fever and El Puerto margaritas, were regularly protesting in the Wayside parking lot and business for Leo, at least for now, was good.

I drove by the next afternoon to see for myself.

Pushed right up against Leo's promenade, huge and unsightly and flanked by the planters he'd bought in the fall, which were still empty, was one of those snow mounds that refuse to melt and seem to change physical properties as the season progresses. It was soot black with some fabric poking out of it, a couple of crushed cans, a shoe, and some silver tinsel. It seemed crazy that it should still be here in May, but we'd had a late snowstorm and temperatures had been chilly. Leo was out with a few of the guys from the kitchen throwing salt at it. One of them brought out a pot of hot water, and then another one. I watched from my car for about ten minutes and in that time, between the salt and the water, they brightened it up and managed to reduce its height by about a foot. I could tell from his posture Leo wasn't happy. I felt sorry for him. Icebergs all over the world were shrinking, but not this thing.

On his second postcard he'd written: "We miss you. Come back soon. Leo and the Promenade." Again the picture showed the yew, in a different season and at a different angle, but there it was.

THE NEXT MONDAY I took the postcard with me to El Puerto. The restaurant was busy, but after a short wait Leo seated me at a table on the promenade. When he brought my burrito, I had the postcard out on the table. I put my finger on the yew.

He smiled. "So it is the right one. Your father said you loved that tree."

"He did?" I was surprised my father would share that. "Did he say why?"

Leo shook his head. "I thought I had the wrong evergreen when I didn't hear from you."

"He told me you might lose the restaurant," I said.

Leo closed his eyes. "Yes. Maybe. We don't know yet. There are some protests being planned."

"I noticed your pots. I could plant them, if you'd like."

He smiled but said, "Flowers won't help."

"Flowers always help," I said.

Leo gestured at the postcard. "What is special about that tree?"

"It's hard to explain. Have you seen it?"

"I don't get onto campus much." The extension class he was taking wasn't even on campus, but in a community center north of town. "But I could."

I told him I was going on another visit soon.

"Are you leaving this weekend?"

"No."

"Well then. Sunday?"

LEO BROUGHT A BACKPACK with a picnic packed inside. He spread a blanket and gestured for me to sit. He took out two iced teas, some fruit, and two carefully wrapped sandwiches.

While we ate I told him the story of the yew, where it came from, how I'd acquired it, how I'd taken care of it. I pointed out the sheltering Sitka spruce. I even told him about the growth rate, which didn't seem to surprise him. He was suitably impressed by all of it.

"The sign is wrong," I said.

He squinted in its direction.

"This is a male yew. There are no berries on a male yew."

"Yews can be male or female?"

I nodded. "And this one's male."

"Then why—"

"Some evidence suggests that the Fortingall Yew is becoming female—one small branch at the top has produced berries—so the university lawyers said the sign had to cover all potentialities."

"But this yew is male?" Leo pointed at my yew.

"Yes. And the yew in Scotland is changing sex only after three thousand years."

"That's ridiculous."

"I agree."

We ate in silence for a while. "My grandmother loved to garden," he said. "Every summer she filled these big planters and hanging baskets on her porch with petunias."

I held my breath.

"She had huge, cascading mounds of them. Every summer. I don't know how she did it."

"Probably Miracle-Gro," I said.

He looked hurt, so I added, "Or maybe she had a way with them."

"I love petunias. I thought they might work in the pots around the promenade. What do you think?"

I almost told him what it was like to spend an afternoon planting petunias, but stopped myself.

"It's nice you have a happy memory of your grandmother," I said.

When we were finished eating, I showed Leo some of the other campus gardens. At the crescent rose bed, I stopped to smell a floribunda rose. Leo waited, then leaned over to smell the exact same flower, as if, despite all the blooms around us, I had found the best one.

Travel Supplies

Route 23 is like a lot of roads leading into towns that tightly zone their historical cores. It's the spare room of the house, the place where you put everything you use only once in a while but aren't willing to give up entirely. It's where you keep your car dealerships, your fast-food joints, your Costcos and Sam's Clubs. Usually there's no pedestrian life at all, it's just a chute for cars running errands.

That's what I was doing when I stopped by the CVS before heading to the train station on my way to New York to visit Vanessa. I was trying to hurry, but a woman started talking to me near the travel-size products.

"I used this brand once," she said. "I liked it."

She wasn't exactly talking to me, but she wasn't not talking to me either. When you suspect a stranger wants your attention, anyone's attention—just a moment of the universe's time—but you avoid eye contact or keep walking, is that being a good neighbor? I wonder what they'd say on the message board.

"I don't know, I don't know," she muttered. "How many ounces are allowed? And is it per bottle or combined?" She wasn't looking at me. She was looking at the little bottle she was holding. But there was no one else around.

I picked out a tiny shampoo and looked at the floor. "Per bottle," I said. "Each bottle can't have more than three ounces."

"Is that right? Thank you. I haven't flown in so long and I know there are all these new rules."

I smiled, sort of.

"I'm really nervous, to be honest."

I believed her.

"Thank you so much. I really don't want to go through one of those full-body scanners. My friend says they're not safe and I had a mastectomy last year. She says you can get in a line for the other kind of scanner. Is that right?"

"I think so."

"Do you travel a lot?"

"Not really. Well . . . recently I have been. I'm leaving on a trip tonight, but by train, not airplane." It's possible this was the most information I'd ever voluntarily given to a stranger.

"For work? What do you do?"

"I'm a botanist."

"Oh, so plants and flowers?"

"Yes."

"That's interesting."

Nevertheless, she had nothing else to say about it. She raised her little shampoo in a kind of salute.

I raised my bottle in return and we parted.

At the checkout there were a lot of registers but only one with an employee behind it. The line was long and forced through an aisle made of candy. I placed myself squarely behind a mother using too many words to encourage her young son to make better choices about what he ate. She in turn was behind a mother with two older children busy on their devices. When the first boy crowded the other two, his mother said, "Make sure to leave room for your friends."

I thought for a moment they all knew one another, then realized she was using "friends" to mean people in your way whom you don't know. The three children eyed one another.

MY TRAIN WAS NOT UNTIL SEVEN, but I got there early because there's a bar I like in the station. It has a white linoleum floor, shares space with a Chinese buffet, and is perennially decorated for Mardi Gras. I don't know why. What I do know is that a small chicken fried rice goes surprisingly well with a glass of cold white wine.

I opened my purse to pay the bill and found a tree sheet.

American Elm (*Ulmus americana*)

In the nineteenth and early twentieth centuries, the American elm was a common street and park tree because of its rapid growth, tolerance of urban conditions, and broad umbrella crown. But overplanting of the species, especially in residential areas where the high, graceful archway over the street was prized, led to an unhealthy monoculture that left the species open to pests and disease.

My parents lost an elm in our backyard to Dutch elm disease when I was young and my father had followed the development of new disease-resistant cultivars ever since. There was one, the Valley Forge elm, that seemed to be doing well in trials. That's probably what he had in mind.

I'd followed the story of the American elm located in a parking lot directly across the street from the Alfred P. Murrah

Federal Building that survived the Oklahoma City bombing that killed 168 people. It was damaged in the blast—fragments lodged in its trunk and branches—and was almost cut down for evidence. But nearly a year later, the tree began to bloom and so was named the Survivor Tree and left alone.

American elm (*Ulmus americana*)

IV

— Hostess Gifts —

"Happy is the house that shelters a friend," Emerson wrote, which is interesting given his decidedly mixed feelings about how long Thoreau stayed with him.

On its best behavior, I might say. But I don't have a lot of personal experience. We didn't open our home easily to others. Being a good host is all about anticipating need and we didn't have the energy for that. And we didn't visit much because being a good guest requires knowing how to let yourself be welcomed. We weren't good at that either.

There are some great party hosts in literature—Fezziwig, Mrs. Dalloway, Jay Gatsby—but few who have to consider the care and feeding of visitors for a night or more. Mrs. Wilcox of *Howards End* comes to mind, but she spends most of her time in the garden and then dies. Maybe the point is you can't be a good host and be present. Bad hosts, however, can drive a story. Think of Goneril and Regan, Roderick Usher, and Mrs. Danvers.

It is Martha, I think, who should be the patron saint of hosts. "As Jesus and his disciples were on their way, they came to a village where a woman named Martha opened her home to them. She had a sister called Mary, who sat at the Lord's feet listening to what he said. But Martha was distracted by all the preparations that had to be made. She came to him and asked, 'Lord, don't you care that my sister has left me to do the work by myself? Tell her to help me!'

"'Martha, Martha,' the Lord answered, 'you are worried and upset about many things, but only one thing is needed. Mary has chosen what is better, and it will not be taken away from her.'"

The "one thing" is faith, of course, which you can't eat or sleep on. So Martha went back to the kitchen. She deserves a gift.

In descending order, the best approach to hostess gifts is as follows:

1. Something for the hostess.
2. Something for the house (which is really something for the hostess).
3. Something for the family.
4. Something perishable.

Something for the children (if there are children) is an altogether separate consideration. But fair warning: children are picky.

— Staging —

On the train to New York, I tucked myself into a window seat. The older woman who took the seat next to me had a short perm and a purple leather handbag and wanted to know where I was headed. It was Memorial Day weekend and she asked if I was off for a "girls' holiday, too."

"No," I said. I thought I said it nicely, but she dug for a long time in her purple bag, and at the first stop she smiled at the air, said, "I think I'll just get a cup of coffee," and never came back.

I had considered driving, but the truth is, much as I enjoy driving Bonnie, I don't love long car rides. The solitude has a way of loosening memories, and when they start to unfurl I'm at risk of being blown off course. Better to take the train, where I can watch the trees rush by, though so many were in bad shape from pruning and storms, they started to make me sad. Do trees regret their lot? The ones struggling in cities or growing along forgotten margins? Do they dream of dark nights and quiet forests?

I was on the high-speed train, but for a time we kept pace with a delivery truck that had a giant scoop of mint chocolate chip ice cream painted on its side. This seemed to me to capture both the degradation of American travel and the American obesity epidemic all at once. After a while, I fell asleep. When I woke up there were two girls, probably late teens, sitting across from me. One was in a red crewneck sweater and drank water from a red thermos she pulled from her backpack. The other wore a blue crewneck sweater and had a blue thermos. They shared a snack of grapes and cheese they had carefully stored in Tupperware containers and spoke quietly to each other in a language I couldn't identify as they passed things back and forth. Between the way they moved together and the color coordination, they were mesmerizing. The young believe the world was made for them, that all of history leads to now, this moment on a train with your friend exploring the world. I thought of Maris and Helen from the café and I had to look away quickly when they caught me staring.

VANESSA NEVER WORE MAKEUP except lipstick, which she loved in deep shades of red, and somehow this was all she needed to bring out her dark eyes and excellent cheekbones. Since college she'd dated a series of dashing and charismatic men who ultimately, after varying lengths of time, had a different sense of the word *commitment* than she did, and although I was not her primary confidant, I believe her heart had been broken more than once. Vanessa's parents had the longest, most stable of marriages. I remember her mother as present and reliable, with a pantry stocked with snacks for us. We were always welcome at her house, and yet of the three of us, Vanessa had been unsettled the longest; she hadn't lived in one place for more than three years. When she married Richard, twelve years her senior, she welcomed into her life twin, eight-year-old stepsons, Colby and Sean, and a Labrador named Shadow.

People rarely like to be reminded of what they once thought, so I had no intention of saying I remembered she'd once planned for a cat and no children.

"I was sure Shadow would be black," I said, trying to settle the energetic yellow dog greeting me.

"Oh, May," she said. "Her name is the least of my problems."

The new family was preparing to move. The apartment, decorated almost entirely in shades of white and cream, had been "staged" for sale, meaning it was Vanessa's unenviable task of keeping house for an unknown duration to the standards set by an exacting real estate agent. Furniture had been rearranged, walls had been painted, items had been brought in, including framed artwork and expensive throw pillows and succulents in white pots. There was a giant bowl of lemons on the kitchen counter, more than anyone could use in a year, and ferns in the bathroom, the same color as the brand-new folded towels. Everything was exceptionally neat and clean, even the boys' rooms, which was creating palpable tension.

"It's all about 'show-don't-tell,' the real estate agent says." Vanessa sighed. "She's supposed to be very good."

Vanessa explained that all of this had come about suddenly, or she would have warned me.

"The boys were going to be with Richard's mother this month, but her plans changed." She seemed carefully neutral about this.

"Would it help if I booked a hotel room? That is not a problem."

"No! I would never forgive myself. Lindy wouldn't forgive me either. She said you two had the best time."

"We did."

"Isn't her house pretty?"

"Beautiful."

"Too quiet for me, but you know I love cities." She poured us each a glass of wine and pointed to the balcony. "Let's sit outside before the boys get home."

The evening was chilly. Just as it had been unseasonably warm when I visited Lindy in December, it was now a cold June in New York. The apartment was on the sixteenth floor with a view of the Hudson and the coast of New Jersey. An occasional seagull soared by. We sipped our wine and Vanessa handed me a printed weather report for the days of my visit, along with a list of things she thought I might like to do while she was at work.

"I have a weather app on my phone," I said.

"Well, I wasn't sure. I wasn't sure you had a phone."

"This is so organized," I said, trying to reconcile the more spontaneous Vanessa I remembered with the printout.

"I have to be," she said. "This staging thing is killing me. Even the pantry has to be kept with everything turned label out because apparently people open cabinets when they're looking for a place to live."

"What?"

"The agent says people need to know what it feels like to occupy the space."

I stared at the river. The news was full of refugees and tent cities and boats full of terrified families fleeing war, and fortunate Americans were walking through immaculate apartments opening other people's cabinets. I tried to bend this image into something kinder, but it wouldn't budge.

We knew Richard was home when we heard Shadow's nails slipping on the wood floor as she raced to him. When we stepped back into the apartment, Richard looked up from the dog and said, "The third musketeer at last!"

"We've been having such a nice time," Vanessa said.

Richard shook my hand. "V tells me you play the flute."

This was confusing, and as I was still weighing the three musketeer comment, I took a sip of wine before answering.

"I played the viola a long time ago," I said.

"I told you," Vanessa said to Richard. "Lindy and I played the clarinet, May played the viola."

"V has been looking forward to your visit. You've been such a good friend to her."

This didn't seem completely right either. I looked at "V," but she was looking down at the stove. I noticed she'd highlighted her hair.

Richard excused himself and disappeared into the apartment. The twins, who had come in with Richard, greeted me politely and went to play a video game in the living room. Vanessa refused to give me something to do in the kitchen, so I wandered back out to the balcony and tried to enjoy the view.

When I got cold, I came in and insisted on setting the table. Vanessa described how the sleeping arrangements would work during my visit. The apartment didn't have a guest room, so the boys were going to bunk together, Colby into Sean's room, and I would have Colby's.

"Sort of like Lindy's accommodations," Vanessa said, jokingly, "but with less space and more Legos."

Shadow would not stop jumping on me (I assumed she smelled Hester, but Vanessa said she liked me). I tried to be jolly about it, but finally Richard reappeared and closed her off somewhere in the back of the apartment, which made both her and the boys despondent. We could hear her whining and pawing at the door.

"Fancy tonight," Richard said, picking up one of the dinner plates.

"Don't be silly," said Vanessa. "We get these plates out all the time."

"Do we?" he said.

"Were they a wedding gift?" I suggested. "You are still newlyweds, after all."

"Oh, no. V just wants to impress you."

Vanessa made a face at him.

"Americans aren't very good at having houseguests," he said. "You know, in Polish there is a saying, 'Guest at home, God at home.'"

"Yikes," I said. "Are you Polish?"

He shook his head.

When we were all at the table, Vanessa raised her glass and made a toast. "To fortnight friends!" she said. She looked exhausted.

"Cheers," I said, and complimented the dinner before I'd even tasted it. It seemed like the least I could do.

Richard said nothing about the food and got up after a few bites to put on some classical music that made Sean and Colby snicker. When he came back to the table he asked them to name the composer, but they couldn't.

"Beethoven?" Vanessa guessed.

"No," Richard said.

"Richard knows a lot about music and is teaching the boys," Vanessa explained.

I nodded.

"Brahms," Richard said, but didn't seem interested in telling us anything more.

We didn't stay up late. Vanessa and Richard had to work in the morning, and the boys left early for school. I fell asleep easily, but in the night was awakened by an unfamiliar warmth against my back. Shadow had nudged open the door to Colby's room and jumped up on the bed with me. I considered pushing her off but worried she might bark, and I didn't want to wake anyone up. I shifted to give myself a little more room, but that left me with just a sliver of blanket. Shadow raised her head and looked at me, completely silent, eyes wide. Then she sighed and dropped her head to the blanket again. She was warm and content and I thought maybe I could be, too. I put my head back down on the pillow. I lasted a minute, then got up and spent the rest of the night in Colby's chair.

THE NEXT MORNING I left a note for Vanessa in the kitchen. I thought it might be best if I got out early and found my own coffee. Shadow seemed to agree but was devastated when I slipped out the door without her. I could hear her whining until I reached the elevator. I hadn't slept well. In addition to Shadow, a few things in Colby's room had beeped in the night, and I'd had the general sense of a lot of small, menacing figures all around me. When I got up to use the bathroom, I'd stepped on a Lego brick in the dark and my foot was still sore.

It was a cool, windy morning. In a café that played surprisingly loud music I bought a cup of coffee to go, made my way to Washington Square, and found a bench. A pigeon that looked like it had had a rough night, too, paced back and forth in front of me. His feathers were clumped and dirty and one of his eyes was infected. Meanwhile, between paving stones nearby, a tiny wild chamomile (*Matricaria discoidea*) was blooming. Plants always beat animals in the ability to thrive in inhospitable environments.

When my coffee was finished, I walked a few blocks south until I came to a garden called Time Landscape. It was meant, according to a marker, to be a "living monument to the forest that once blanketed Manhattan Island." The north end contained a little woodland of oak, white ash, and American elm, then there was a small rise toward a grove of beech trees in the center. The south end had the grasses, birches, and wildflowers of a young forest.

We preserve old buildings, why not old landscapes? But wilderness on that scale didn't make a lot of sense. It was enclosed on all four sides by an iron fence and there were no benches. It was like a zoo enclosure without the animals and it made me feel lonely. Trash was blowing in, leaves needed to be cleared, and one of the cedars was leaning precipitously. Another had a man's necktie draped over a branch.

I was about to go when I noticed a woman working near the beeches. She was tiny, gray haired, and wearing wool from head to toe.

"Visitors on Sundays," she said.

"Are you the gardener?" She had a shovel and a rake, work gloves, and a watering can. There was no shed in the garden, so her tools were leaned against the trees.

"One of them."

I could not see how she had gotten in, but there must have been a gate somewhere.

"Visitors on Sundays," she said again.

I didn't answer, and after a minute she looked up from her work to see if I was still there. "You can also donate time or labor." She stretched her back.

"Isn't that the same thing?"

She studied me.

"Labor is time, right? How would you donate time to the garden without labor?"

"Up to you," she said. She took a drink from her watering can and turned back to her work.

"I might if I lived here," I offered, but she didn't answer.

On my way back to Vanessa's, I paid more attention to the city trees. I saw bark scraped off by scaffolding and trucks, broken branches, and twisted trunks. On one corner I saw three desperate-looking honey locusts (*Gleditsia triacanthos*) next to a Starbucks. Two were festooned with torn balloons, the third had a tattered plastic bag stuck in its branches. All of them were suffering from too much salt in the soil.

Horrified, I said out loud, "These trees are being poisoned!"

But no one around me stopped or asked what I meant or how I knew. One of those sudden city whirlwinds came up and caught a plastic cup in the street. It made a sound like tap dancing against the asphalt until it was crushed by a passing car.

At a farmers' market I bought a bouquet of wildflowers for Vanessa. When I got back to the apartment everyone was gone for the day. I put the flowers in some water and went to Colby's room for a nap.

———

THAT EVENING VANESSA hired a babysitter for the boys, and we went to a Chinese restaurant for dinner. After a day apart, Vanessa and I were happy to be in each other's company. We told stories about the past, ostensibly sharing them with Richard, but we were really just talking to each other. He didn't ask a lot of questions, but neither did he interrupt, which was nice. The privilege of the closest friends in the group seemed to be keeping him quiet. He perked up after Vanessa told me she'd recently run her first half marathon. He told me he'd run three plus one full marathon. "Richard is a great runner," Vanessa conceded. And when Richard was disappointed about not being able to try two different dishes, Vanessa changed her order to accommodate him. I was surprised, but maybe I don't understand the pleasure of compromise when you're in love.

When we opened our fortune cookies, mine said, "Redecorating will be in your plans."

Vanessa wasn't impressed. "In New York that's like saying breathing will be in your plans."

"But I don't live in New York."

Richard read, "'Whistle while you work.' That's a command, not a fortune."

"Do you?" Vanessa asked.

"Never."

Vanessa's said, "You will soon cross the great waters," which made her shake her head. Then she looked at me. "You're going to London soon. You take this one and I'll take yours. I could use it for the new apartment."

I didn't think fortunes worked that way, but I was more than happy to play along.

On the way home, I asked if Shadow might be able to sleep somewhere else that night. Vanessa was horrified. "Oh my god! Why didn't you say anything?"

"Everyone was asleep."

"May. Of course. We'll put her in with the boys. I'm so sorry."

"You could have pushed her off the bed," Richard said.

"I didn't want her to bark," I explained.

"May's nice," Vanessa said.

"Oh, does she keep dollar bills folded in her pocket, too?"

Vanessa rolled her eyes, hugged her coat around her, and walked faster. We pulled ahead of Richard on the sidewalk. "I hate it when he makes fun of me. I do that so it's easier to give them to people on the street."

"Why?"

"I don't know. It's easier. I'm embarrassed to take my whole wallet out."

But I'd meant, Why is he making fun of you? When we were young, I'd felt at times I was Vanessa's project. She was more socially adept and took me under her wing—literally. She would reach her arm around my back to pull me in for a side hug, my far arm pinned, but it made me feel cared for, protected. Now I did the same to her.

———

THE NEXT DAY we set out to see the High Line, but it started raining before we got there, so when we arrived at the Gansevoort entrance we ran into the Whitney instead. Vanessa quickly found and was mesmerized by a modular, portable living space called *Living Unit* by Andrea Zittel. The artist's statement said she'd been inspired by the fine line between freedom and control, and how people often feel liberated by parameters. The piece was set up in a corner far from a window and looked like a cross between a large wardrobe and a closet. It was meant to contain everything needed to make a life:

2 mugs

2 cups

2 bowls

2 mirrors

a toaster oven

a stovetop

1 pot

1 skillet

4 storage jars

4 hangers

2 folding chairs

1 folding cot

2 file drawers

a desk calendar

I stood next to Vanessa wondering why she was so fascinated.

"I keep trying to think of what else I would absolutely need," she said.

"I would need at least one flowerpot."

Vanessa looked at me. "You really like plants."

I shrugged.

"Okay. So you can use one of the storage jars for an orchid or something."

Other people came over for a while, but no one stayed as long as we did. One woman with well-cut hair, stylish glasses, and trendy jeans stood with us for longer than I expected. I was sure she had a sofa at home she was very proud of.

"What do you think Lindy would make of it?" Vanessa asked.

Vanessa and I didn't have a history of talking about Lindy, so I wasn't sure if her question reflected a difference in the way she was thinking about me or Lindy. "Not cute enough," I said honestly.

She nodded. "Yeah, but she'd fix that."

"What about books?" I said.

"Lindy's are organized by color."

I pointed at the *Living Unit*. "I mean where would they go? There's some space above the desk. You just wouldn't be able to accumulate too many."

A round-bellied man in a baseball hat and running shoes came by. He looked for a few seconds, then turned to us. "How does it work? Where are you supposed to put it?"

"It's supposed to make us think," Vanessa said.

He wandered off.

"Do you think it could work for a family?" Vanessa asked.

"Maybe if you doubled the number of glasses and chairs."

"I was looking at a furniture catalog the other day and it said, 'Your living room is where you share the story of who you are.'"

I hesitated.

"I'm texting a picture to Lindy," Vanessa said. Under the picture she typed: "New apartment!"

Lindy responded almost immediately. "Perfect! I'll make curtains. Say hi to May."

Vanessa texted something back, then put away her phone.

"You two are good at staying in touch," I said.

She nodded. "We talk pretty often. Not long, just five minutes here and there."

I didn't like the phone very much, but I was trying to understand.

"What can you say in five minutes?" I asked.

"Oh, it doesn't matter. The conversation is ongoing."

We moved for a tour group assembling around the *Living Unit*.

"I'd like to stay in better touch," I said.

"You're going to change now?" Vanessa laughed.

"Can't I?"

"You just are who you are, May. I understand if I don't get a Christmas card from you in, what, fifteen years? It doesn't mean anything."

"It really doesn't. You're my friend."

"I know. Come here," she said. The clasp of my necklace had come around the front and was hanging next to the pendant. "Make a wish," she said, fixing it for me, something she'd done all the time when we were young.

"Let's cheer ourselves up with a glass of wine," she said.

But there were no tables available in the restaurant; most were occupied by well-dressed pairs of women drinking wine.

Bowls

O n my last night Vanessa made dinner. Sean was in his room, Richard would be home late, and Colby and I were sitting in the living room holding books. Vanessa had sent me to read with Colby, which relieved that visiting stress of wondering what I should be doing, but Colby was not reading and neither was I because in the kitchen Vanessa was talking to her mother on the phone and I was trying to hear the conversation. They had a casual, daily relationship that intrigued and baffled me. They discussed some upcoming plans, made arrangements for a visit after I was gone. When Vanessa's mother realized I was there, she told Vanessa to give me a hug, and Vanessa did. She walked into the living room with the phone in one hand and a wooden spoon in the other.

"She's right here, Mom. Okay, I'm hugging her. My mom sends her love."

"Me, too," I said, truly touched, my throat tight.

Vanessa smiled at me and squeezed my arm, then walked back to the kitchen. "Okay, Mom, I've got to go. Love you. I'll call you later."

I felt like I'd just seen a blue whale or a shooting star. I blinked back tears, then looked at Colby, who was holding his book, the cover closed.

"Don't you like to read?" I asked.

He shrugged.

Vanessa walked halfway back into the living room, the phone gone but the spoon still in her hand. "Have I told you about my friend who makes the bowl paintings?"

"I don't think so."

"Oh, she's something, the kind of person who can manage everything at all times. When she decides you're a true friend, she makes a bowl painting on a small, square canvas and hangs it on a wall in her living room. The bowl represents you and when you visit, you have to guess which bowl you are."

"Are you up there?"

Vanessa laughed. "She's painting me now!"

"A wall of bowl paintings."

"Yep."

"Can I just start with sending Christmas cards?"

Vanessa laughed and spun around to go back into the kitchen.

"Books are your friends," I said to Colby. He frowned, but I thought this was an important message after the bowls. "'There is no friend as loyal as a book.' Ernest Hemingway."

He seemed unimpressed, but he opened his book, which I took as an encouraging sign. I went to the kitchen.

"How's your mom?" I asked.

"Busy. I can't keep up with her. She volunteers, goes to shows. She's leaving soon to study Spanish in Costa Rica for a month."

I must have looked sad because she hugged me. "I loved your mom," she said.

"Did you?"

"Yes, of course."

"What do you remember?"

"Oh." She set down the measuring cup she was holding. "Well, I remember how she would watch movies with us sometimes and talk to the characters on the screen. Remember that? She could be really chatty sometimes, then at other times, very quiet."

"Yes."

"I remember the picture she gave us for graduation."

"Do you still have it?"

"On my dresser in the bedroom."

I waited, hoping for more.

"Didn't you two walk together a lot?" she asked.

"For a little while."

"I thought that was nice. My mom and I didn't do that then."

Vanessa turned back to making dinner. This is the problem: conversations like this, where one is more deeply invested than the other, can be frustratingly staggered and incomplete.

Vanessa hadn't done anything wrong. She simply had no idea how much the information meant to me, and, of course, it was dinnertime. She was juggling a lot of things; I wanted something pure and complete and true.

She fed the boys first, then we ate while they did their homework. She looked over at the table where they'd left their messy plates and sighed. I wanted to mention my mother again, but then Vanessa said, "After the move I'm getting a kitten. A neat, little girl kitten. Then, with Shadow, the boys won't outnumber the girls." She smiled at the dog that was curled at my feet. "Will you come back to see our new place?"

I leaned over to pet Shadow. "Will it be as white?" I asked.

Vanessa laughed. "Richard says it happened after the twins were born. Their mom was sure they were going to be girls and had bought a lot of pink: clothes, bedding, furniture. After the surprise of the boys, she redecorated everything in white." She gestured dangerously with her glass, full of red wine, at the apartment.

"That's a little spooky," I said.

"I know. I hope I can make a good home for them. Their mother is so distant." She sounded uncharacteristically melancholy.

"Homes do have to be made, don't they?" I said.

"I'm trying to figure it out."

"Me, too," I said.

"Are you and your dad still sharing the house?"

"Yes."

"It's been a long time, May. Could you at least renovate?"

I laughed. "That really doesn't feel like an option."

"I'm sorry. I know it's hard for you."

"How are you?" I asked. "How are you . . . settling to it?"

"Life with the boys?"

I nodded.

"I love it. I really do." She paused. "Can I be brutally honest?"

"Brutally?"

She smiled. "Honesty is always brutal."

"Okay." I thought she was going to say something about herself and the boys, but she asked, "Why are you still single?"

"Why are you married?" I shot back without thinking and was genuinely sorry when she didn't say right away, Because I love him. She didn't say anything for a while. The rims of her eyes grew red and she took a sip of wine. "We're trying to have a baby," she said finally.

"Lindy thinks I'm sad because I don't have children, so maybe you're both right."

She smiled. "Lindy is very kid-centric. We had a picnic in Central Park with them not too long ago. She made me hold the baby for an hour. It was exhausting. Somehow I ended up entertaining all the kids while she and Max took the afternoon off."

I stayed quiet.

"Anyway," she said in a tone that meant "enough." She looked around the apartment. "I'm not going to miss this place. I am going to miss the building, though. The doorman is wonderful. Do you know he gave up complaining for Lent?"

It felt late in the visit to start something new, but to my surprise I did. "There is someone in Anneville."

Vanessa was shocked. "Wait, what? There is someone? Why didn't you tell me sooner? Why does all the good stuff come out on the last night?"

"We've had a picnic. Well, one picnic and two postcards. That's it."

Vanessa looked so happy, and some of the tears she'd seemed to be holding back started to spill out. She crossed her legs on the sofa. "Postcards? That's romantic. No one writes postcards anymore. What's his name?"

I PACKED BEFORE BED that night and straightened the room as best I could, but it's hard to know how to leave a room you've borrowed from an eight-year-old boy. I didn't think Colby and Sean would be wild about the bumblebees I'd brought, so I'd purchased a couple of Lego sets for them and left those on Colby's desk. I was proud to have thought of the idea, actually. I hoped it gave them a good impression of their new stepmom's friends.

I tried to make myself sleepy by staring at the glow-in-the-dark stars on Colby's ceiling (in no discernible constellation I could see), though I couldn't stop thinking about the *Living Unit*. I admired its simplicity, but it wasn't a home. As much as I'd like to deny it, a home does tell a story—in fact, it should—because the question of what you want to own is closely related to how you want to live. I climbed out of Colby's bed and tiptoed back into the living room, took one of the real estate agent's little white pots, and flushed the succulent down the toilet. I don't care for them and there was no way to get it home anyway.

I rinsed the pot in the sink and stepped out of the bathroom. It was strange being up at night in someone else's house. Though I suddenly felt like an intruder, I walked into the living room. I could hear the ebb and flow of traffic on the West Side Highway, nearby someone honked, then there was a yell. The apartment had windows on three sides, a glass box, allowing views into the buildings on either side. It was past one and most of the windows were dark, but in one room a woman was watching television. I couldn't see the screen but it must have been very large because the bouncing blue light in the room looked like a tempest.

Behind me I heard footsteps and Vanessa's voice somewhere near. "Well. You know. May." Three full stops; its own kind of shorthand. I didn't know if she was on the phone or talking to Richard. Whoever it was—Lindy? her mother?—the person understood because she didn't have to explain further.

But I wanted to say, "Wait. No, I don't! What?"

Her voice moved deeper into the apartment and I stood for a moment holding my breath, looking at the pots on the balcony, planted beautifully by someone. I was pretty sure they had a balcony landscaper. I'd seen the van parked in front of the building earlier. I wanted air, but I couldn't figure out how to open the balcony door and there was no way I was prepared for the ordeal of hallway, elevator, and doorman, even one with a

knack for self-improvement. I opened one of the windows—
they were giant and slid left and right instead of up and down—
but the child-lock system allowed only about two inches. I
leaned toward the gap and breathed the cold air. I would have
planted lilac (*Syringa vulgaris*) on the balcony, but, then again,
the sixteenth floor might be too windy for it.

Back in Colby's room, Shadow was asleep on the bed.

— Clapham Common —

The next day I found myself again in an airport with time on my hands, but this time it was JFK. I'd made plans to fly directly from New York to London to see Rose because the airfare was cheaper that way. Vanessa had put me in a cab to the airport.

"Call me," she said. "Sometimes?"

"I will."

"Will you?"

"I will try."

She blew me a kiss as the cab pulled away.

At JFK I sat at the gate for a while. There were several TVs in the area, but most people were looking down at their own phones or laptops. Half a dozen people were reading magazines, one person was holding a book, and there were two knitters. I admire the knitters. You can pretend to be reading, but you cannot pretend to knit. Also, it takes a lot of commitment to cart the supplies around.

When the flight was delayed, I found a bar and ordered some food and a Bloody Mary. The TV screens in the bar were, as usual, split between sports and violence, but this time the sport was baseball and the violence was against people protesting the newest travel ban. I followed the choppy closed-captioning while Muzak played over the airport speakers. A journalist was discussing the idea of America and how its meaning around the world was being diminished. At the end of the bar there was a man wearing one of the red baseball caps, but he had earbuds in and was watching something on his phone.

I checked my bag at the gate. Grendel miraculously fit in the bin, as always, but the flight was full. The attendant behind the counter looked tired and sad. "You look reasonable," she said, and asked if I would be willing to check my bag for the sake of the flight. How could I not agree?

And so I arrived in London, but Grendel did not. I gave the airline all the information they wanted—name, local address, phone number, one unique identifying item in the bag—and they told me I would "almost certainly" have the bag back within twenty-four hours.

"Almost certainly?"

"The bags we find we find quickly."

"And the bags you don't find?"

"They are not returned within twenty-four hours."

"That seems accurate," I said.

I named Emily Post as my identifying item, which pleased me, but I had to spell *etiquette* for the airline representative.

ROSE LIVED IN A BUILDING on a street called The Pavement along the east edge of Clapham Common in south London. Her apartment was over two rival estate agents on either side of a gelato shop, and she had a bay window overlooking a paddling pool. "Rose on The Pavement" she was fond of saying, and it was also printed on her business cards. She worked as an independent landscape architect. Her niche was designing beautiful yet functional vegetable gardens. Her only regret was that her apartment on the fourth floor didn't allow her to have one of her own. For eight years she'd been waiting for an allotment on Lorn Road, where allotments were in such high demand the waiting list was closed. "At least I'm on it," she said. "Now I just have to figure out who to kill."

Her apartment had a great view of the common and lots of dappled sunlight that filtered in through the trees. There were two rooms: a bedroom painted gray and a long open-plan living and dining room. Edith Wharton disliked the open plan, feeling it was forgetful of the individual uses of each room and contributed to a woeful loss of privacy. She deplored the widening of doorways into arches, referring to them as "yawning gaps." But I thought Rose's space was inspiring. The living room half was painted a dark ochre; the kitchen/dining half had many different paint splotches in various places because Rose was still trying to decide on a color and everything from pale pink to jade seemed to be under consideration. She asked my opinion as soon as I arrived, but I didn't have one. All the colors seemed miraculous to me. To be honest, I didn't even know one was allowed to paint rooms those colors. My family had always followed the "white makes a room look bigger" school of design, but I don't know why that's important. Sometimes you don't want a room to feel bigger. Sometimes cozy is better.

Rose didn't have a lot of furniture, but there seemed to be a comfortable place to sit wherever it was needed. There was a good long table for eating at one end of the room, and a Victorian daybed for resting at the other. She had a beautiful mission-style desk and a number of mismatched chairs she'd found at estate sales that nevertheless managed to look like they belonged together. Edith Wharton would have delighted in her commitment to good furniture over cheaper, mass-produced pieces.

Mainly Rose had books. Her shelves were tall and industrial and she'd carted them with her from place to place even though they were heavy and impractical. The books were shelved in roughly alphabetical order, sometimes three rows deep. She was the kind of person who had multiple copies of the books she loved most. That way, she said, she could always give one away.

The Victorian daybed doubled as a guest bed and I had doubts, at first. But then Rose pulled out a three-part screen to give me privacy from the kitchen end of the room and brought out an enormous armful of soft blankets and pillows. She helped me make up the bed and by the time she left me, I was more comfortable than I thought possible. It's true I was jet-lagged, but I don't think that fully explains the quality of sleep I enjoyed that night. I went to bed in one of Rose's T-shirts, and in the morning she had a pair of jeans for me to borrow and a soft white sweater that was similar to something I had at home, but in gray.

After we met in the Landscape Architecture program, Rose and I discovered we'd briefly lived in New York at the same time, though Rose was more like Amber Dwight. They probably would have been friends. For example, Rose had grown two lemon trees in her tiny apartment bathroom because she was living above the canopy line and missed dappled sunlight. So she made it herself with the lemon trees, which had to be kept in the bathroom for the extra humidity.

"Wouldn't a ficus have worked just as well?" I'd asked. "And you could have kept it in the living room."

"First of all," she said, "it was a studio apartment, so there wasn't a living room. Second of all, lemons."

But lemon trees are notoriously fussy. One of our professors in the program used to warn us about getting too attached to our plantings. Careful research into soil, drainage, and sun exposure was all part of the job, but if the plant didn't thrive, we had to let it go. "It's important to accept plant death," he would say.

"Bullshit," Rose said, and claimed nothing had ever died on her watch.

WE HAD COFFEE AND TOAST for breakfast and then Rose said we were going to visit a historical house. I feel about historical houses much the way I do about biographies: guilty I don't enjoy them more. I might even say I'm allergic to them and other small museums. So much attention to the maintenance of so little invariably makes me gloomy. And if the person died in the house, all the worse. Rose wouldn't tell me which one we were visiting.

"It's a lesser-known gem," Rose said as we walked. We turned into a square north of Fleet Street and she dropped the cigarette she'd been smoking. Her smoking started as a rebellion against the excessively healthy lifestyles of the other students in our graduate program, but the habit stuck. "I grow healthy vegetables," she'd say. "It'll balance out."

There was a house on the corner with a blue plaque, but first Rose guided me toward a bronze statue near the middle of the courtyard.

"Hodge!" I said. Samuel Johnson's cat. He sat on a thick book, a few empty oyster shells in front of him, and an inscription quoted Johnson: "a very fine cat indeed."

"Rose, this is perfect!" I hugged her, surprising us both.

"The collection is thin, but I thought you'd like to see the garret where he worked on the dictionary."

That the collection was thin was, to me, the root of its charm. Most of the original furnishings were dispersed after his death, and the room set up as the library had probably been, according to a notice, his bedroom, so there was no bed to see. Johnson took nearly nine years to complete the dictionary, though he'd claimed he could finish it in three. It was finally published in

1755, and until the completion of *The Oxford English Dictionary* 173 years later, it was the preeminent dictionary in English and still ranks as one of the greatest achievements of scholarship ever produced by one person. We stayed more than an hour, a record for me, and had lunch at a nearby pub.

When we started back to her apartment, I got a text from Vanessa. It was a picture of the chalkboard in their kitchen, on which someone had written "May Rulz!" Vanessa texted, "Colby wrote it. They loved the Lego sets. You now have coolest friend status."

I showed Rose. "Is that your friend in New York?" she asked. I nodded.

"Is she the one who always wears outfits? You know, matchy-matchy."

I thought she probably meant Lindy. "No. That's my friend in Connecticut." It was true, Lindy's style would not have been to Rose's liking. But when people are asked what is most important to them in a friendship, the top two answers are consistently loyalty and kindness. "She has good reasons for wanting to appear put together," I said, and started to put my phone away.

"Aren't you going to text her back?" Rose asked.

I pulled my phone back out and Rose watched while I typed, "I've never been praised with a misspelling before. I feel cool."

Vanessa sent back the nerd face emoji and Rose laughed.

Two women about our age passed us just then walking arm in arm. Rose noticed them, too. She dropped her cigarette in the gutter—it's still hard for me to watch her litter—and took my arm. I had never walked that way with a friend. I wasn't sure if it was a block or two arrangement, but our arms stayed linked the rest of the way home.

THE JUNE WEATHER was glorious, but Rose and I didn't do a lot the next couple of days. I can't remember another time when I've been as content to spend so much time inside. It's true I didn't have my own clothes, but I also loved her apartment. It seemed like a space that was completely in tune with the person who lived there. Nothing was arranged for anyone else's benefit, and yet it was easy to be comfortable. Rose kept asking if I was bored and I kept saying no. We made tea and read books and talked. I stared for hours out the front windows, happy to watch the huge black crows hopping around the bright blue edge of the paddling pool. Rose never smoked in the apartment, so when she went downstairs to have a cigarette, I had the place to myself. I probably enjoyed too much pretending it was mine. Rose worked on her drawings and blueprints and once a day we took a long walk in Clapham Common, a thousand-year-old city park with three ponds, a Victorian bandstand, and so many beautiful open-growth trees I couldn't pick a favorite.

"You're sure you're not bored?" Rose asked once again on one of our walks. I noticed a banner featuring happy children digging in the dirt. Community gardening posters always feature children, but in my experience it's the old people who do all the work.

I pointed to it. "If I am, I'll volunteer."

"Do you want to see the Tower of London? Most people want to see the Tower of London."

We slowed down to watch an old woman with a walker lean over to raise a bent lily and carefully prop it among its peers.

"I do not want to see the Tower of London," I said.

"Do you want to meet some of my friends? I could host a dinner party."

"Please don't."

"But you're sure we're not being slothful?"

I told her avarice, envy, pride, lust, and wrath harm others, and gluttony is bad for your health. But sloth is just a willingness to move slower than others and that's not a crime. I've always thought despair should be the seventh deadly sin instead.

"Okay, I agree," she said. Nevertheless, she dragged me into the bandstand as we passed and took a picture of me leaning against one of the red painted columns. "There," she said, showing me her phone. "Now you can say you've done something touristy."

Rose collected her mail when we got back to the building. "For you," she said, handing me a postcard and raising her eyebrows.

This time the image was an aerial view of the campus gardens in summer. "You've made it beautiful here," Leo had written. "I hope you won't forget."

MY BAG ARRIVED THE FOURTH NIGHT, not within the twenty-four-hour period suggested, but I didn't care. The airline called at ten o'clock to say the bag had been found and would be delivered within the next two hours.

"Will you be awake?" the woman asked.

"What if I'm not?"

"Then we make arrangements to deliver it tomorrow. We cannot leave the bag at the door. You must receive it."

I asked if she could guarantee the two-hour window.

"I can guarantee that it is in a car on its way to you."

Rose went to bed and I stayed up reading, hoping for the best. A few minutes before midnight, I heard the buzzer. The driver spoke with a Russian accent.

"Are you the bag seeker May Attaway?"

"I am." I tried to buzz him up, but he didn't open the door. His voice came through the speaker again.

"I can't come up. I'm afraid you have to come down."

I slipped on my shoes and coat and took the elevator. Outside the front doors of Rose's building there was a man in a driver's cap standing beside Grendel. I thanked him.

"I'll need you to prove your identity," he said, and made a sound that seemed like a sneeze, but it ended in a giggle.

"Really? But you brought the bag to this address, which is the address I gave the airline, and here I am. Who else wants a suitcase at midnight?"

"You'd be surprised."

"I don't have my wallet. I'll have to go back up."

"Is there something unique in the bag you can name?"

"Yes, I already did that. I have a copy of Emily Post's guide to etiquette. It should be right on top."

"Let's take a look." He was wearing a gold silk tie and a nice suit. The driver's cap was a little grubby, as if part of a different uniform, and on the street behind him he'd left his car running. He giggle-sneezed again, then lowered Grendel to the pavement and opened the zipper gently. He peeked inside, then closed the bag and handed it to me.

"Very good. Here you go." Another sneeze.

"Thank you," I said again. "And thank you for driving out at night. You have a cold."

"No, no. We did you the disservice. And everyone wants the bag immediately."

"Is that right?"

"I don't mind. I like putting people back on track. Good night!" He hurried back to his car and disappeared. I went back upstairs and was in bed before it occured to me that the car had been very fancy for a messenger. A Jaguar? It seemed at least possible I'd received some divine help.

London Plane (*Platanus acerifolia*)

The London plane tree arose as a chance hybrid between two foreign trees, possibly at Oxford, in about 1670. One parent is the Oriental plane, *P. orientalis*, from Turkey; the other is the American sycamore, *P. occidentalis*, from the eastern United States.

The bark is smooth and grayish brown and peels off in puzzle-shaped pieces to reveal a tan or pale green trunk beneath. The reason for this unusual adaptation is the bark's lack of elasticity; the outer layer cannot expand as rapidly as the tree inside it. Trees take in oxygen through their bark as well as their leaves, so it turns out this bark shedding allows the plane to thrive in air pollution. For this reason it is planted in cities all over the world.

While I applauded my father's embrace of such an adaptable tree—not to mention his perseverance and cunning; this tree sheet was folded into an outside pocket of Grendel—the fall foliage of the plane is notably unspectacular and the abscission, or leaf drop, is late and sudden, a torment to landscapers. I know what Blake thinks of the ones we already have on campus, and I didn't want to be responsible for adding another.

Pilgrimage

At dinner the next night I told Rose about my friendship-themed gift ideas, the honey pot and my latest: fridge magnets with Eudora Welty's "Friendship is inherently a magnet" on them. She ran to find her copy of *Bartlett's Familiar Quotations* so we could flip through the quotes on friendship and find some more.

"'I would have friends where I can find them,'" she read, "'but I seldom use them.' Emerson."

"Coasters," I said. "No one ever uses coasters."

"Yes! Perfect. 'How few of his friends' houses would a man choose to be at when he is sick.' Samuel Johnson."

"One of those tissue box cozies."

"Yes."

"I would happily stay here if I were sick," I said.

"You are welcome, in any state, any time."

I thanked her.

"You okay?" she asked.

I nodded.

"Are you going to tell me about that postcard?"

I smiled. "He's a good friend."

"Hmm, I don't think that's the whole story." She squinted at me. "May, do you have a garden?"

"I have the whole university."

"I mean at your house."

I said I'd planted some things over the years, but nothing had thrived.

"Exactly," she said. "What about that yew you planted? How's it doing?"

"It's getting tall."

"Hold on. Where was that cutting from again?"

"Fortingall."

She stared at me.

"In Scotland," I added.

"I know it's in Scotland. May, why aren't you going up there to see it? You have to go see it."

"I don't know. I came to see you."

"How can you be this close and not go up there?"

I didn't know, by which I mean I was surprised the idea hadn't occurred to me.

Rose was muttering under her breath, something about pilgrimages being important. "You have to go," she said again.

"Would you come with me?"

"Really?"

I nodded.

Rose tilted her head and waited, giving me a chance to back out. When I nodded again, she jumped up. "Let me check." She looked at her schedule on her phone. "I'd have to bring some work, but yes, I could do it."

I don't know how to explain it, but suddenly we had wind in our sails. I changed my return flight while Rose booked us a flight to Scotland and found a place for us to stay. "May, the Fortingall Hotel is right next to the churchyard where the yew is!" she called out, still on the phone.

I arranged a rental car while she packed a bag (including, among other things, her gardening gloves and a trowel because she never left them behind) and we were ready to go by midnight. A detour, and yet I'd never made a decision so quickly in my life.

WHEN JAMES BOSWELL, Johnson's friend and eventual biographer, wanted to deepen his friendship with Johnson, he proposed they travel together. They went to the Western Isles of Scotland, remote and difficult terrain where they often had to sleep in tents, and once, a cave. The endeavor made our cushy Scottish plans seem trivial by comparison, but the concept was sound.

Rose and I flew from Stansted to Glasgow, then drove north to Perth. I adjusted to driving on the left more quickly than I thought I would, and thanked my mother for her good training. We followed the A9 to Ballinluig, then took the A827 west to Aberfeldy. From there we took the B846 to reach Keltneyburn, then turned up the single-track Glen Lyon road to reach Fortingall. It was a long and exhausting journey, but if Menelaus was blown off course on his way home from Troy because he hadn't made sufficient sacrifices to the gods, I was getting off easy.

I could see the yew behind its wall when we arrived even though it was after dark. I'd looked at so many pictures of it online, I knew exactly which shape it was.

The concierge said, "Here to see the yew? One of the oldest living organisms in the world." She'd obviously said it ten thousand times.

"We are," Rose answered cheerfully.

"We're full up with pilgrims at the moment. Always are in June."

"How many of them have a cutting from the tree?" Rose said, pointing at me.

The concierge raised her eyebrows in my direction. "Really. Well, that is interesting."

I turned to Rose. "I think I'll just walk around a little now."

"Go," she said.

The tree's once massive trunk, measured at fifty-two feet in circumference in 1769, is split now into separate stems, giving the impression of several trees. This is a result of the natural decay of the ancient heartwood, which would establish its true age. Nevertheless, modern estimates put the tree somewhere between three thousand and five thousand years old. It's protected by a stone wall, but in 1833 a caring local noted that branches and even some of the trunk were still being removed by travelers to make drinking cups and other curiosities. A sign on the wall reads, simply, THE YEW.

I walked in the road next to the churchyard for a while, content to look from a distance. In spite of Rose's encouragement, it still felt like a long way to come to see a tree. I went closer, but the gate in the wall was locked. Indignant, I put my hands on my hips, then leaned my forehead against the bars until I was cold.

When I got back to the hotel, Rose was smoking outside the front door. "How'd it go?" she asked.

I shrugged. "The gate was locked. I'll try again tomorrow."

Rose stamped out her cigarette, hesitated, then picked up the butt. She wiggled the door handle. "Oh, no," she said. "We're locked out."

"Oh, my god. This is not going well."

Rose smiled. "Just kidding. The concierge gave me the key. She's a smoker, too. Thank goodness for people with bad habits," Rose said.

Our room was clean and bright, though Grendel barely fit between the wall and the end of the side-by-side twin beds. I wanted the bed closer to the window, but hesitated. Rose threw her backpack on the bed closer to the bathroom.

"Go ahead," she said. "This is your pilgrimage."

"But I wouldn't be here without you."

"True."

Rose used the bathroom first and when she stepped out, her long blond hair was braided down her back. She reminded me of a character in a Victorian novel, except for the black sweatpants and tank top. I changed and used the bathroom, too, and then we turned out the light.

In the darkness I realized this was the first time I'd ever

traveled with someone who was not family. I smiled with my eyes closed.

"What are you thinking about?" Rose asked.

I opened my eyes. We were each curled on a side, facing each other across the little aisle of carpet. Rose's eyes were wide open.

"Go to sleep," I said.

"I can't. It's too quiet. I'm used to London."

I got my phone and went through a number of white noise options. She picked "rainstorm" and I plugged the phone in between us.

"Perfect," Rose said, and we both fell asleep.

THE NEXT MORNING was cloudy and cool. I thought the church might be empty, but after breakfast Rose and I found a team of older women already decorating for Sunday. A few other tourists were sitting and watching and the women didn't seem to mind, so we sat in one of the pews, too. The flowers they were working with were mostly white and yellow: camellias, daisies, lilies, goldenrod, and meadow buttercups. They were adept at making beautiful arrangements and worked slowly and quietly, stepping back often to survey the effect. Most dipped a knee toward the cross every time they passed in front of it. They all wore trousers and cardigans even though it was warm.

After a while, Rose got up and went over to one of them. They talked quietly for a few minutes, then the woman gave Rose a white camellia, which Rose brought back to me.

"She says you're welcome to go out the back of the church and see the yew."

"You're good at pilgrimages," I said.

The others in the church must have been pilgrims, too, because after seeing Rose and me walk out the back, they followed until there were about a dozen of us in the small compound around the yew. We stepped slowly, plotting our paths so as not to bump into one another, dipping our heads in acknowledgment if we came too close. These were my people, but I still wanted them to go away. It took some time, but eventually they all drifted out until Rose and I were alone with the tree.

I would challenge anyone who has ever used the term "tree hugger" in a derogatory manner to stand in the presence of a three-thousand-year-old yew and not feel something. Those branches will beckon. Our primate ancestors spent longer in the trees than our relatively young species has spent on the ground and the trees still welcome us; they remember.

I'm aware not everyone feels the way I do about trees, but I have no idea why not.

The compound was smaller than I'd imagined, the shade colder and darker. The oldest part of the tree had lost most of its heartwood, leaving a cavernous space I wanted to sit in, but markers on the ground suggested we weren't supposed to get that close. From the time we'd come in, I'd been pacing around the area slowly. Now I stopped.

"Do you want to talk?" Rose whispered.

"Not right now," I said. "If that's okay."

Rose nodded.

In bonsai you often plant the tree off center in the pot to make space for the divine, a practice I respect with no real feeling for what it means. Standing near the yew, I understood. It was as if the silence around the tree were deeper than it should have been, the colors denser. If someone had told me there was a presence there protecting the yew, I would have believed it. Yews were considered sacred for centuries, still are by many gardeners. Yew hedges can withstand even the most merciless cutting back and recover as though nothing had happened. Low branches can form new roots and grow into trees where they touch the ground. Beams made of yew may sprout again long after they've been built into houses. The Japanese have a word for the calming, restorative power of simply being in a forest or among trees: *shinrin-yoku*, forest bathing. I was in the presence of only one tree, but it was enough.

I glanced at Rose, relieved she knew all this, too. I didn't have to explain. I still didn't want to talk, but I thought of how Rose had gotten me to Fortingall and I wanted to try. "I feel like I should say something, but I'm at a loss."

"Me, too."

"I planted the yew for my mother."

"I've wondered."

"Her ashes are . . . I planted it with her ashes."

"Oh, May."

"I've never told anyone. Except my father. He knows."

"Oh, May," Rose said again, and covered her eyes with her hand. Then after a minute she looked up. "I memorized the Lord's Prayer a long time ago. Do you want me to say that?"

I shook my head.

"We are in a churchyard," she reminded me.

I smiled. "True." But I had remembered some lines I'd memorized from a poem by Wendell Berry about a sycamore and said them out loud.

"It has risen to a strange perfection
in the warp and bending of its long growth.
It has gathered all accidents into its purpose.
It has become the intention and radiance of its dark fate."

Then, I must admit, I waited. I hoped for a breeze or a bit of birdsong—something that would acknowledge my presence. I've always wanted the pathetic fallacy—the idea that the natural world takes an interest in our affairs—to be true. Sometimes the signs are clear: rain falling on the president at the inauguration. Other times the indifference is haunting: a clear September day filled with death.

Standing in the churchyard before the yew, I got nothing. No wind, no rustlings, just quiet. After a while, I smiled and touched a branch and told Rose I was ready to go.

"That was perfect," Rose whispered as we walked through the gate.

At a pub in Fortingall, we ordered pints and sat at a small table outside. The sun was struggling to come out. I usually dislike a midday clear, by which I mean I like consistency. I prefer a day to finish the way it started, whatever the weather.

But Rose was delighted and her enthusiasm was contagious. A waitress about our age was wiping off tables, which were damp from an earlier shower. When a small group of young friends came up, she greeted them affectionately.

"When'd you get home?" she said.

"Yesterday."

She beamed at them. "You brought the sun with you."

My camellia was on the table between me and Rose. "I'm going to press this," I said.

"Do you want to buy any postcards?" Rose asked mysteriously.

I smiled. "I'm going home tomorrow."

"True," she said.

I hadn't given Rose a gift yet because I'd planned to find something for her in London. Back at the hotel I saw a drawing of the yew in the gift shop and I bought one for her. A little later I went back and bought another one for me.

ON OUR LAST NIGHT in Scotland it rained and the cars along the road outside our room were loud on the wet pavement. I slept fitfully and dreamed I was walking over lots of broken pieces of something—a collapsed house was my sense but the pieces were small and mostly white and everything was covered in the masonry dust you see in footage of bombed-out cities. The pieces crunched a little underfoot and I was walking toward my father but he was angry and shouting at me to be careful, to look where I was stepping. I immediately fought back and said it was fine, I wasn't going to do any more damage, was I?

I described the dream to Rose at breakfast and her eyes filled with tears.

Perhaps a best friend is someone who . . . holds the story of your life in mind. Sometimes in music a melodic line is so beautiful the notes feel inevitable; you can anticipate the next note through a long rest. Maybe that is friendship. A best friend holds your story in mind so notes don't have to be repeated.

Rose wiped her eyes. "Are you sure you shouldn't move out of that house?"

"I think I'd rather learn how to live there."

"But you've given it a good shot."

I nodded and blew my nose and wiped my eyes. "Why are we friends?" I asked. "I'm older, I was depressed when you met me. I can't help your career or introduce you to anyone."

"May."

"What?"

"You really want to do this? Fine." She smoothed her palms on her lap. "I like the way you work. You're kinder than you think you are. You're sad and a little grumpy, but so am I. I don't know. You're making me think too hard."

"Sorry."

"This feels like a eulogy."

I laughed. "Exactly. That seems to be the only time we summarize our friends."

"Because it's the best time."

"Why?"

"Because certain things only come into focus when a person is gone. It's sad but true. You need memory and loss to polish your thoughts. Otherwise you're just writing a speech or an introduction or something."

I didn't know what to say.

"You don't agree? What does Johnson say? How does he define *eulogy*?"

"No, I agree with you. But if you were going to describe me to another friend of yours, and you wanted to give her an impression very quickly, the way people do when they talk about their friends to other people, what would you say?"

Rose tilted her head and stared at me. Then she looked down. I thought I'd stumped her, when she looked up and said, "Prickly, but in a soft, long-needled way."

"I like it."

"Good," Rose said. "Now what about me?"

I knew immediately. "Tall and determined and evergreen, like arborvitae."

"I'll take it."

We took a selfie before we left Fortingall. I feel about the word *selfie* the way Johnson felt about *finesse*, "an unnecessary word, creeping into the language." Nevertheless, we waited for the procession of churchgoers to finish, then stood by the wall around the yew, our cheeks touching. Just before the picture, the wind blew a strand of Rose's long hair so that it wrapped over my shoulder, and I thought maybe that was the sign I'd been waiting for. Two people, side by side, looking straight ahead. I think C. S. Lewis was onto something. We don't have music to reveal the direction of our lives, of course, but if we did, I'm pretty sure mine would have soared just then.

We flew back to Stansted and I had to get straight into a taxi to Heathrow for my flight home. We hugged and promised to stay in better touch. I got into the taxi and waved as it pulled away. A few minutes later, I got a text.

"Miss you already," it said, followed by a tree and a heart emoji.

I regret the loss of real correspondence and am not a fan of the text. But if a certain poetry is being lost, perhaps a sense of immediacy and presence is being gained. Those words and, yes, those pictures right then made me happy.

"I miss you, too," I wrote back. And after a minute, I added a tree and a heart emoji, and then a sun, and pressed send.

A few minutes later, Rose texted back. "May Attaway? Using emoji? Oh my heart."

It had been almost nine months since I'd gotten my leave. I'd visited four friends and one tree and had five days left. I wasn't sure what to do with them, but it was only June and I had until October to figure it out. To add to my windowsill, I had a couple of Rose's pens and paint-chip cards. I also had the yew etching. I planned to hang it in the front hall when I got home. I was afraid it was going to look small in the otherwise bare space, but it was a start.

White oak (*Quercus alba*)

V

V

⸺ Settling ⸺

Landscaping lights illuminating the undercanopy of a willow. An old wisteria vine winding up the front of a house. Robins still foraging in the dim evening light. My redeemable element game was going well. In front of a well-restored Arts and Crafts bungalow painted in shades of brown, I saw a man getting his newspaper. We'd half smiled at each other many times on my walks through Duck Woods, but had never spoken.

"Good evening," I said.

"Evening," he replied.

"This house was run down when I was growing up," I continued, to his surprise. "I used to believe it was haunted."

"Really?" he said.

"You've done a lot of work."

"We have."

When I didn't say anything else, he looked back at his house as if to check. "The painters just finished yesterday, actually."

A robin, triggered by the streetlight flickering on, began to sing.

"It looks nice," I said.

"Thank you." He seemed genuinely happy to hear it.

"Well, have a good night," I said.

"You, too."

Rose keeps above her desk a copy of a photograph of French soldiers in World War I standing in front of a small vegetable garden adjacent to their trench. They did not have to build it. They were not ordered to plant a garden. I figured it represented for Rose an image of hope or optimism in the face of odds, but when I asked her, she shook her head. "It reminds me there is beauty in contrast."

As I walked away from the man in the brown bungalow with the perfect yard, I thought the idea would make no sense to him.

But who knows? I'm tired of judging.

Why do I like gardening? Because I worry I've inherited a certain hopelessness, a potentially fatal lack of interest, that I'm diseased with reserve. Making a garden runs counter to all that. You can't garden without thinking about the future.

It's odd that Penelope didn't garden, though I appreciate her lack of interest in decorating. She changes nothing in the house while Odysseus is away, but when he returns, she orders his bed to be moved outside the bedchamber. Odysseus knows the bed can't be moved because he made it himself and one of the posts is formed from a living tree. In this way she tests his identity. The tree roots them to their house, where they settle once again.

Settle. The word gives me pause. You can settle a dispute and you can settle into a life. In its transitive form it means "to place so as to stay."

I suppose what you are reading is my attempt to settle. There's a story I've been trying to tell, one about friendship and friends and what place they have in a life, and one I've been trying not to tell about my family. Does that make me an unreliable narrator? To a certain extent, aren't we all? We don't get to write from scratch the whole story of our lives. We are given certain plot points that must be incorporated. Maybe we settle when we've done the best we can.

Is it real? I once asked Amber. What? she said. Your life! The things that happen to you. Is it real or are you just really good at making it all into stories? She said, I don't understand the difference. —Alice

Transformation

We no longer perceive metamorphosis in our world in the way Ovid wrote about it, but when my mother took to her bed, she was neither sick nor well, neither dying nor continuing to live the life she had. What else defines metamorphosis?

What my family lacks is a story.

I believe my mother tried to contain her sadness by withdrawing and growing root-bound. When a plant outgrows its container and isn't repotted into a larger one its roots grow round and round, halting growth. Just so, my mother got her children to the brink of adulthood, then her roots began to grow round and round, tighter and tighter. But mortals cannot decide how much pain is enough. So Atlas, god of endurance, punished her. Her pain grew until it bulged out of her. The first repair surgery failed. So did the second. The bulge grew and grew until eventually my mother's left side looked as though she had a pillow under her shirt. Or a newborn swaddled there.

Then the hernia grew some more until it was so large her arm couldn't hang straight but fell in a curve as if around a child's shoulders. The surgeons said, Give science ten years. And so she waited, the caretaker becoming the cared for. She changed from someone who gave hugs to someone who didn't like to touch or be touched. The hernia, filled with her own intestines, locked her into an awful embrace with herself, a diabolical punishment for a person who had always struggled to believe she was lovable.

"I love you," she would say, even before she was sick.

"I love you, too."

"Do you?" She needed the repetition like a drug.

"Yes! I love you very much."

Even when the exchange went as she hoped, she looked sad.

Where was Eleos, goddess of pity and compassion? Or Artemis, reliever of disease in women? Or even winged Hermes, god of thresholds and boundaries, who might have softened her fall?

WHAT HAPPENED ISN'T COMPLICATED. It doesn't take a long time to tell. When I came home after college, I moved back into my old room, which was the largest. The house didn't have a master bedroom with a bath, just the three bedrooms and one full bath on the second floor. My large room was originally the room my brother and I shared when we were young, my parents had always had the midsize room, and the smallest bedroom was my brother's. With my mother's health in decline, my father was more often than not sleeping on the sofa downstairs. We thought they'd both be more comfortable if we moved her to my room, and I would take the downstairs guest room until I found my own apartment.

I emptied my closet and drawers. I boxed up my books and Steiff and glass animals. I went to a department store and bought my mother a new bedspread, picking one with lavender hues I thought she'd like. My father and I changed the bed's orientation so that it would be easier for her to get in and out from either side. He built a little wooden step for her, hoping that would also help. My brother bought a beautiful old mirror for over the dresser, which reflected the opposite window and added to the airiness of the room.

When everything was ready, we filled the bedroom with flowers. It was August. My mother liked it well enough, as much as she liked anything then. Misery loves company, they say. My mother kept her shades drawn against the sunlight most days. She reveled in the TV news, all of it evidence that the world was rotten and she wasn't missing much. With pain and depression her personality was changing.

It's not a complicated story. One warm September evening we had dinner, I can't remember what we ate, and my mother went back up to her room right afterward, as usual. I cleaned the kitchen while my brother went up to do his homework. My father played Beethoven's *Pastoral* Symphony, loudly, so my mother would hear it upstairs. It was their favorite. I had another glass of wine. My mother had been in her new room less than a week.

It doesn't take a long time to tell. In her old room, the place where she'd slept with my father for twenty years, her path in the night to the bathroom was out the bedroom door, turn left, three steps, turn right into the bathroom. That night, after we'd all gone to bed, she came out her new bedroom door, took three steps, and turned right off the top of the stairs. The night was moonless and dark. Because of the hernia she was misshapen, off balance, and wobbly on her feet. She must have been on her way to the bathroom. I've paced it out a thousand times.

Everybody trips on stairs at one time or another. It's actually been calculated that you're likely to miss a step once in every 2,222 occasions you use a staircase. The two times to take particular care are at the beginning and at the end because most stair accidents occur on the first or last step. Not surprisingly, going downstairs is more dangerous than going up. More than 90 percent of injuries occur during the descent. When did humans decide we needed staircases in our homes? When and where did one floor become insufficient?

My mother fell nine steps to the landing and her head went through the balustrade overlooking the front hall. Her nose was broken, several teeth were knocked out, and there was a lot of blood. Her neck broke on impact, they said, but I know I heard her. It didn't sound like her, but there was a sound.

The ambulance was not quiet when it came.

I have wondered: Did the *Pastoral* Symphony that night make her sad? Did it remind her she might never walk again across such landscapes? Which of us decided we should move her to my bedroom? We can't remember. We won't remember.

There was no funeral or memorial service and each of us healed around the tragedy the way a tree grows around a rock. My brother finished his senior year, got into a California college, and flung himself across the country. I didn't blame him. He'd done his job. The parent he'd had his eyes on in the car was still alive.

My father moved to his basement apartment and I moved into my brother's room and cleaned and covered the blood stains in the hall. No one came to visit or help. But I didn't ask them to. I started gardening. That first spring I found a surprising number of shiny pennies on the ground, which signifies only that I was looking down all the time. Sue has a penchant for finding four-leaf clovers, but no one in my family has ever been that lucky.

Are we a family damaged beyond repair? I don't know. I do believe in the power of words and stories to make sense of things.

I can still hear my mother's voice: "You'll be fine without me."

Well, we are and we aren't.

— Ginkgo (*Ginkgo biloba*) —

G*inkgo biloba* is sometimes described as a living fossil because it is the sole survivor of an ancient group of trees older than the dinosaurs. It is the only member of its genus, which is the only genus in its family, which is the only family in its order, which is the only order in its subclass. That's pretty lonely, which is why I think it should be forgiven the fact that its seeds when fallen smell like vomit.

This seemed like a brave choice on my father's part.

Recently Chinese scientists published a draft genome of *Ginkgo biloba* showing the tree has an exceptionally large genome of 10.6 billion DNA letters (the human genome has 3 billion), enabling a huge number of antibacterial and chemical defense mechanisms.

The greatest examples of the ginkgo's tenacity are in Hiroshima, Japan, where six trees growing between one and two kilometers from the 1945 atom bomb explosion were among the few living things to survive. The Japanese have a word for them, *hibakujumoku*, trees that survived the blast. The six trees, though charred, were soon healthy again and are still alive today.

— Hester —

One night last week I was late getting home from work because I stopped to do some errands in Barracks Mall. Afterward, in a rare lapse, I couldn't find my car. Bonnie was in Leo's shop, so I was driving my father's Taurus and he hates the fobs that make the car honk and flash for you. I like to think of the mechanism as similar to a horse snorting and stamping for its rider, but he doesn't agree.

"How many times in one life can you remember where you parked your car?" I've asked him.

"I intend to find out," he says.

I usually park in the same spot if I can, near the landscaped island closest to the Barnes & Noble, but if it's not available, I have a few rules. I tend to the right, I tend toward shade, and I will not park next to anything larger than a Jeep. I don't mind walking so I never worry about proximity to the shops and feel sorry for the circling people who do.

When I finally found my father's car, it was sandwiched between two giants: the one and only Hummer in town and a Chevrolet Suburban. I was tempted to key them both, but I didn't. I have never vandalized anything and I didn't want to start.

When I got home, I put on Chopin's nocturnes to calm my nerves and started dinner. After a while, I realized I hadn't seen Hester. She usually wanders into the kitchen to wait for her dinner. I put out her food and called, but she didn't come. I checked her usual places, but she wasn't in any of them. The only windows open were the ones with screens. Still, a worry started to grow.

The house on Todd Lane has old-fashioned windows with sashes and separate heavy storm windows that are supposed to come off in the summer for the screens. Then, ideally, the screens come off in the fall and the storm windows go back up. It's a lot of work and I haven't done it in years. The screens are stacked in the garage, most of them rusted. I just keep the screens on one window in the kitchen and one in my bedroom for fresh air when I need it.

I started moving through the house fast, oddly aware of the disconnect between the beautiful nocturnes and my search. I looked everywhere, in the closets, beneath the beds, on top of the towels, behind the sofa, every single one of the secret places I knew Hester liked. I opened kitchen cabinets, wondering if she'd gotten stuck inside somehow. I even opened the refrigerator. I called her name over and over. I thought she knew the word "treat"—I kept a pouch of them around for her—so I grabbed the bag and ran through the house shaking it, repeating "Hester, Hestia, treat, treat" until I started to cry. I called Sue, who had been taking care of Hester when I was away. I thought she might know if Hester had a new secret place, but she said when she checked on Hester she was usually asleep on the couch.

"I can't find her," I cried.

"I'll be right there," Sue said, and hung up.

When the doorbell rang, I was amazed that Sue had made it over so fast, but I opened the door to find Janine holding Hester, who looked only mildly agitated.

"I found her in the backyard when I went around to drop something off for your dad. I didn't think you let her out, so I scooped her up and took her home with me. She's a sweetie."

I reached for Hester, who was, gratifyingly, squirming a little bit to get out of Janine's arms.

"Are you okay?" Janine asked.

I couldn't speak.

Sue pulled into the driveway. When she saw me holding Hester, she rested her forehead on the steering wheel for a moment before opening the car door. "Thank god," she said, coming over. She scratched Hester's cheek, then pet my shoulder.

Janine and Sue introduced themselves, and while we stood there on the front step, they managed to discover they had a mutual friend. Someone named Ned who did odd jobs.

"How did she get out?" I said.

Janine said she thought the kitchen window screen might be loose. We walked around the house to see and she was right. The screen had come out of the frame.

"I think she must have been sleeping on the sill and just rolled out," Janine said, petting Hester, who was still in my arms. Hester must have been a little rattled because she didn't usually allow herself to be held for so long.

"Good thing it was on the ground floor," Janine said.

"May doesn't take her storms down," Sue said, and Janine and Sue looked at each other as if they had a mutual understanding about me.

"Okay, Hester," Sue said. "Tell your mama you deserve extra treats tonight. Are you okay?" she asked.

I nodded. "Thanks for coming," I said.

"Of course. Anytime," she said, and squeezed my arm.

Sue left and Janine offered to help me get my storm windows down in the spring, if I wanted. I said that would be nice. Then she offered to help me wash them, too.

"We could even get the outsides done now, if you wanted," she said.

I told her I would think about it.

Night Gardening

Recently it has been popular to say that Emily Dickinson gardened at night because for a few years in middle age the sun stung her eyes. I feel certain it was more complicated than that. The woman was a recluse. Her garden was important to her thinking and being out there at night would have given her a chance to think while invisible, not just to the world but also to her family. She stayed away from people so she could be herself and when she was in the garden at night she could be another self, which is, interestingly, Aristotle's definition of a friend. Something about the night work appealed to her.

The ice mound in front of the El Puerto promenade was long gone, but it was July now and Leo still hadn't put anything in his planters. I didn't know if he was discouraged or disinterested, but I did know I hadn't encouraged him and I wanted to fix that.

I went to my favorite nursery, the Garden Keeper, which is

down a hill from a new development of enormous houses. Sometimes I drive around up there and check on some of my favorites, like the house that looks like a stone castle with a veranda. It's the first house on Ski Club Drive, though there isn't a ski club in Anneville.

Today, though, I pulled straight into the Garden Keeper's lot. I knew from my father that the rehabilitation center across the street was where Beth Gould was recovering from her stroke. I left Bonnie running while I considered driving over to visit her. I wouldn't be able to do it after I bought the plants because they'd wilt in the trunk. I sat for several minutes, ultimately deciding I wasn't a close enough friend. I pictured Beth surrounded by all of her real friends, the ones who gave her the silver plate, and turned off the car. I decided I would send flowers when she was home.

The university receives most of its plants from several large commercial nurseries, so there was no need to frequent the local places and I hadn't been to the Garden Keeper in some time. The day was hot and the cicadas, the sound of surf for the land-locked, were thrumming. In addition to disliking petunias, they are a flower I have never been able to grow well. They get long and spindly on me. Nevertheless, I was determined. I greeted the flats of them respectfully and asked that we give each other another chance. A light breeze ruffled their thin petals.

Edith Wharton's philosophy of room decoration matches mine on container gardening: "Concerning the difficult question of color, it is safe to say that the fewer the colors used, the more pleasing and restful the result will be. A multiplicity of colors produces the same effect as a number of voices talking at the same time." I bought three flats of Easy Wave shell pink petunias plus a small English boxwood (*Buxus sempervirens "Suffruticosa"*) for the center of each pot to provide vertical and year-round interest. For texture I bought some creeping Jenny (*Lysimachia nummularia*), which cascades beautifully and its golden, coin-shaped leaves would pick up the yellow centers of the petunias. It was a simple but elegant design, I thought, just like Leo's promenade.

ALL THE WAYSIDE SHOPS were closed when I drove into the parking lot that night. It was midnight and traffic was sparse; the summer students weren't yet partying. Streetlamps cast cones of light through the humid air and I could hear crickets and peep frogs in the dell. Leo had added a couple of strings of fairy lights over the promenade early in the summer, but they were off now.

Everything I needed was in my trunk, so I backed up to the planters and got to work. A few cars drove into the lot, probably hoping someone at El Puerto would still make them a burrito, but they left quickly when they saw it was closed. One car stayed awhile, and I thought maybe someone was watching me garden. When the engine switched off, I looked up and saw a couple of students making out in the front seat.

I was placing the last pale pink petunia in the second planter, my back to the parking lot, when Leo said hello. I jumped straight into the air.

"I'm sorry!" he said. "I didn't mean to scare you."

"What are you doing here?" I must have sounded angry.

"I was working late in the garage," he said defensively.

I scrutinized the darkness in that direction.

"In the office. Paperwork."

I nodded.

"When I saw someone over here, I grabbed a flashlight."
He shined the light on the pots.

"You said your grandmother had petunias."

"She did. They were pink."

"I guessed."

"Good guess," he said.

"I like pink. I don't like red, but I like pink." I looked
around. "Well, I'm all finished. I was just about to clean up.
The plants are small now, but if they're happy here, they'll trail
over the sides by the end of the summer. It should look nice."

"They're perfect. Thank you." He shined his flashlight
on the promenade's red table umbrellas. "You don't like red?"
he asked.

"Red flowers. I don't mind red on other things."

"Oh, good."

Leo aimed the flashlight back at the petunias and we stood
there looking down at them.

"I did like one red flower," I started. "One year my father
brought back a cardinal flower—*Lobelia cardinalis*—from my
grandmother's and planted it behind our house. He tried to ap-
proximate the streambed or lowland environment the plant
needs with a milk carton full of water and a tiny pinhole in the

bottom. It seemed to work for a time." I paused, a little breathless from all the words.

"What happened?" Leo switched the flashlight off and we stood there in the dark.

"He painted the carton green so it wouldn't distract from the garden. It was quite a feat to keep that plant alive in our backyard and he did it for a few years. But eventually he lost heart, or interest, I don't know. My mom started needing more care, I was getting ready to leave for college. It was hard to watch him give up something he'd enjoyed. For a while, I kept the milk jug full myself, but when I came home from school my first summer, the plant was dead."

Leo was quiet.

"And that's why I don't like red flowers."

"When did your mother die?"

"The year after I graduated. I came home that spring, she died in September. She fell down the stairs, but she'd been ill for a while."

Leo shook his head. "I'm sorry."

He helped me put all my gardening supplies back in the trunk. Then we stood next to my car, facing each other.

"Before I went to college, my mom and I drove together a lot, around town and sometimes out into the country. She'd spend the whole day inside, but she'd come out in the evening for a drive with me. Sometimes I drove, sometimes she did. It was nice being in the car with her. We had an easier time talking when we were both facing straight ahead."

"Maybe that's why she wanted to teach you to drive."

For every action there is an equal and opposite reaction, Newton's Third Law of Motion, by which he meant forces come in pairs. With my gift of time from the university, I'd been trying to reach out, as they say, trying to make a family of friends. Just now it occurred to me what the opposite force was, the anchor to my year of visiting.

Leo raised his hand to cup the side of my neck and cheek, a gesture I love in movies, and I kissed him.

Meadowbrook

Protests to save Wayside went on all summer, though without the margarita-loving student presence, they were small. Newspaper editorials in support of construction cited the growing school system and city housing numbers. Editorials in opposition invoked the importance of green spaces and healthy ecosystems. No one knew when or why, but the developer changed his plans. He decided to rename Wayside mall Meadowbrook, make the store signs beige and uniform, and build his condos just in the dell with a thin band of trees left as a barrier.

So the protests to save the dell began. It was discovered the dell was a sanctuary for a certain kind of finch, and also an ancient burial ground for the Monacan people native to the region. Jane Jacobs was invoked, but she wrote more about cities, so that was confusing. Someone proved it was one of only a few remaining habitats for an endangered tree frog. Someone else discovered that the soil they would use to fill the dell came from another state where the trees had emerald ash borer disease, raising the prospect of transporting the beetles across state lines.

On a Friday in early August, local day-care centers and summer camps protested. They arrived by foot or city school bus and made a day of it. A picture in the paper showed a little boy mournfully holding a handmade sign that read PLEASE SAVE OUR DELL while all around him children jumped and somersaulted on the sloping meadow.

Leo didn't want to lose the dell, but everything else was just what he'd always hoped for: a beautiful name and the possibility of an enormous increase in foot traffic. He said the developer was thinking about putting a fountain in the parking lot, and the condominiums were going to be called The Aspires, which the promotional material explained as a new kind of living for an old kind of soul, *aspiration* combined with *spire*.

"Is it a retirement community?" I asked.

"I don't think so," Leo said. "But they're using a lot of stone and wrought iron, and there's a spire."

"One spire."

"That's what the plans showed. The architect said it would be a suggestion of antiquity."

Shear Elegance was closing, which was for the best, and a high-end shoe boutique was moving in. Someone had signed a lease for the empty storefront; Leo had heard it might be a bookstore. Mrs. Kim's Inconvenience had reinvented itself, seemingly overnight, as an upscale country market with local produce, artisanal cheese, a coffee station, and a smile on Mrs. Kim's face. No one knew how she'd done it—though she'd been spotted driving a red convertible V W Beetle—but everyone was glad.

All the last-ditch efforts failed and the developer broke ground, or rather, started filling in the dell, at the end of August, beating the return of the students by days. The following week, Leo got his new sign. We bought more planters for the promenade and a few for the garage as well, though I've told Leo that large hanging baskets over the bays would look nice. He says it's all up to me. The petunias I planted are thriving.

— The First Night-Blooming Cereus Party —

I t would be difficult to overstate how gangly and unlikely the *Selenicereus grandiflorus* is when not in bloom. It's a sprawling, branching plant with a thick, knobby stem meant to clamber up trees or rocks in arid landscapes. In a pot it must be supported by a stake and still it grows around and around and entangles itself. The bud, when it produces one, is nine inches long.

But when it blooms . . . The scent has been described as ambrosia, part orange flower, part vanilla. It is intoxicating, but not overwhelming, not like the scent of lilies, which so many people dislike with good reason. The scent of the *S. grandiflorus* is finespun. It doesn't fill your nose, it fills the air around you, which makes a big difference. The bud grows for weeks, but when it begins to open, the bloom and wither occur within twelve hours. The outer petals are spindly and pale yellow. They open first and fold nearly all the way back. The next layer of petals is a little wider, salmon colored to a pink buff, and they open straight out. The inner petals are white, the stamens thin, and the anther yellow. When fully open, the flower can measure up to fifteen inches across.

I don't know when the bud on the Goulds' plant first appeared. My father had been carrying the plant back and forth between the window in his kitchen and a sunny spot in the backyard. It probably could have endured the summer overnight temperatures, but he was taking extra care. It was early September when he showed the bud to me and it was about to open.

Reader, I planned a party. Quickly and with a lot of help—it was more of a potluck, really—I invited people to gather in my house. The flower began opening at six o'clock and by the time people started arriving at eight, the fragrance was already strong. Leo brought chips and guacamole from the restaurant. Blake's wife brought a cake she'd decorated with flowers, some made with frosting, some real, all of them edible. Sue and Maria brought glow sticks and wintergreen mints for the kids when it got dark. Apparently if you chew on a wintergreen mint in the dark, an observer will see what looks like lightning in your mouth. "It can get a little messy," Sue said, shrugging. "They have to chew with their mouths open."

Janine brought several bottles of wine. Recently I'd learned she was building a tree house in her backyard. I was worried at first because a lot of designs involve putting the house at the heart of the tree, requiring a number of big branches to come off. Her design, however, in order to spare the tree, was a house on stilts, the back attached to the trunk, which acted as a ladder up to a small door. Between this and the wine, she was rising in my esteem.

And Philip Gould brought a pot of blue asters, Beth's favorite late-summer flower. "She never liked to cut flowers," he said.

"I have always felt the same way," I told him.

Two days after I sat in the parking lot of the Garden Keeper and decided not to visit Beth, she suffered a series of additional strokes. She spent a week in hospice care, then Philip moved her home, where she died a few days later in her own bed, surrounded by family and friends. A memorial service is being planned for the spring and Philip has asked my father to speak. When I close my eyes I can see the front of that rehab building. Not going in is a mistake I hope never to repeat.

I put the asters on the floor right next to the night-blooming cereus so we could admire them together.

"That's nice," Philip said, looking at the pot. "Thank you." My father brought him a piece of cake and the two of them talked quietly in a corner of the living room for some time.

I knew of course that my father and Philip were friends. But to see Janine and Sue greet each other warmly? And Leo meet Blake, shake his hand with reverence, and start asking about drought-resistant perennials? A little later, I saw Leo talking to Janine, and my father was laughing with Sue and Maria, and Blake came up to me and said, "Did you know giraffes hum at night? Janine told me." He looked delighted.

I felt warm and stepped into the front hall for air. There were children playing in the front yard. I didn't know if they went with people at the party or not, but I opened the door and told them to come have some cake. All of them came running inside.

Back in the kitchen I found Sue and Leo laughing.

"What's so funny?" I asked.

"You," Sue said, and wrapped her arms around me. "We think you should get local kids involved in landscaping the new Meadowbrook parking lot with nothing but petunias. What do you think?"

"Very funny."

When I'm doing well like this, when things are running smoothly and in balance, I wish my mother could see me. I wish she were sitting quietly somewhere at this party, just watching. I don't want her to be impressed; I just want her to see how it's possible to order a life, how it's possible "to gather all accidents into our purpose." I'd like to show her the pink tape measure, the stone bird, the little white pot, the pressed camellia. Also the hobbled fawn, Leo's postcards, and Rose's paint chips—all the gifts, or contraband, of my visiting year. I wish my mother had had her own, so she could have known what it means when a friend remembers how you take your coffee, or that you don't like scary movies, or what you called your grandparents. I'm still not the center of a group, but if I died tomorrow, Vanessa would plan a memorial service within a week, Lindy would make it beautiful, and Rose would know what to say or read. I'm less sure about Neera, but that's okay. I have more than I need.

I dreamed recently that I had only a few minutes to write something about each of my friends but couldn't find pen or paper. So I started writing with my finger in the sand and everyone gathered around to read. We were staying together in a house by the sea. The dream made me happy because—I'll admit it—I've always loved those books where friends gather for a weekend and lives are changed.

Around nine-thirty the bud was almost fully open and, as it was dark outside, Sue opened the glow sticks and handed out the mints. Some of the children ran outside with abandon, but a few stayed, settling cross-legged on the floor, Henry and Bella among them. They were in awe of the flower, and I smiled watching them. I sat down next to Henry and he turned.

"Thank you for inviting me," he whispered.

"Thanks for coming," I whispered back.

Some of my other neighbors on Todd Lane came, but not many. Maybe next year more will come.

In *Beowulf* Grendel, standing outside alone, was *harrowed* by the din of the banquet, a terrible word meaning "to lacerate or wound the feelings of." Amber Dwight never would have allowed that to happen. I'm sure she would have kept the doors of Heorot wide open.

The Tree That Owns Itself

The last tree sheet. This one I gave to my father.

The white oak (*Quercus alba*) is one of the preeminent hardwoods of eastern and central North America. In the forest it can reach a magnificent height, and in the open its canopy can become massive as its lower branches extend far out laterally, parallel to the ground. The wood has great strength and durability, so the oak has been used in shipbuilding for centuries. Good crops of acorns occur at intervals of a few years, called "mast" years, from the Scandinavian *mat*, meaning "food."

At the top of a steep hill in Athens, Georgia, where Dearing and Finley streets intersect, there is a tall white oak with a stone tablet in front of it that reads:

For and in consideration of the great love I bear
this tree and the great desire I have for its
protection for all time, I convey entire possession

of itself and all land within eight feet of the tree on
all sides. William H. Jackson

Jackson was a professor at the University of Georgia and these words are from his deed to the tree, circa 1840. The tree, which locals today call "The Tree That Owns Itself," fell in a storm nearly a hundred years later, the year my father was born, and a seedling cultivated from one of its acorns was planted in its place.

MY FATHER SAID HE'D WANTED the tree on university grounds because he thought I'd sell the house after he died. But I'm not going to do that. The house on Todd Lane may be the geographical center of our tragedy, but it hasn't done anything wrong.

My father and I are going to visit Georgia next month. It's a mast year, I checked. We'll find an acorn from the white oak in Athens and bring it home, where I'll cultivate the sapling at the university until it's ready to be planted in our backyard.

Grendel wasn't a very expensive suitcase and his miles are showing. He has one mauled corner and a wheel that creaks when it rotates. He looks like he's been in a fight or two, but I mended him with some duct tape and he's ready for another trip. My father says he has a friend we can stay with, which is news to me. I'm delighted.

Leo thinks I should drive, which might be nice. My father and I haven't taken a trip together in a long time and we'd be in new positions in the car. If nostalgia is the recovery of something lost but with a difference, I'm likely to be swamped by it. My father, too. But we're thinking of swinging through Savannah on the way home, where we'd both like to see the Spanish moss. My brother might come, not with us to Georgia, but home for a visit after our trip. A strange expression, *home for a visit*. It's not definite yet, but I'm working on the guest room for him just in case.

His name is Ben.

And our mother's name was Miranda, invented by Shakespeare, derived from the Latin *mirandus,* and meaning "worthy of admiration, wonderful."

Rules for Visiting

1. Do not arrive telling stories about the difficulties of your trip.
2. Bring a gift.
3. Make your bed and open the curtains. A guest room is not a cave just because it's temporary.
4. Help in the kitchen, if you're wanted.
5. Unless you are very good with children, wait until you hear at least one adult moving around before getting up in the morning.
6. Don't feed the pets.
7. Don't sit in your host's place.
8. If you break something, admit it.
9. Say good night before bed.
10. Always send a thank-you note.

There are others, but these are the essentials. They should cover every house and living situation, large or small, rich or poor, cozy or elegant, married or single, children or no children, and every kind of visit, family or friend, local or abroad, long or short. I have very few friends and not one of them is replaceable. May you settle and find good friends.

ACKNOWLEDGMENTS

The writer Amanda Davis, who died in 2003, was beloved by many. I was not lucky enough to know her, but her story affected me deeply, and her attitude toward friendship, as I understand it from the dozens of beautiful tributes written for *McSweeney's* after her death, was the earliest inspiration for May's journey.

Michael Downing, Janice Nimura, Clare Aronow, and John and Jackie O'Farrell are friends, hosts, and early readers of the highest order. Thank you.

The day Edward Carey agreed to draw trees for this book was one of my happiest. Thank you. They are perfect.

Thank you to Sharone Ornstein for all the conversations; Fiona McCrae and PJ Mark for believing in the idea; and Ginny Smith and Laura Barber for deep, insightful editing.

Mitchell, best friend for twenty-eight years and counting— thank you for everything. Olivia, who read an early draft, and Simon, who helped with names—I love you and hope you find many fortnight friends.

Keep in touch with
Granta Books:

Visit granta.com to discover more.

GRANTA

THE REPORT

Jessica Francis Kane

'Fascinating and movingly human' *Daily Mail*

'An utterly authentic journey into a little-known tragedy of
the second world war . . . A compelling, sensitive and
fascinating novel' John O'Farrell

On 3 March 1943, the East End of London braced itself
for an air-raid. No bombs fell that night, but as the crowds
surged towards the shelter of Bethnal Green Tube station, 173
people lost their lives. What happened during those few fatally
confused minutes is the subject of an immediate enquiry, but
for the survivors, it will be years before truth can finally be
disentangled from rumour, and grief from guilt.

'A smart and troubling novel of ideas' *Financial Times*

'The story itself has an appalling fascination, while the restraint
of the telling lends it considerable power' *TLS*

'A spellbinding examination of the blame game' *Vogue*

FEATURED ON BBC RADIO 4'S *A GOOD READ*